LOVE IN THE FORTRESS

LOVE IN THE FORTRESS

Caris Roane

Copyright © 2015 by Twin Bridges Creations, LLC.

This is a work of fiction. Names, characters, places, and incidents are products of the author's imagination or are used fictitiously. Any resemblance to actual events, locales, or persons living or dead is entirely coincidental.

Formatting and cover by Bella Media Management.

ISBN-13: 13: 978-1515022695

THE BLOOD ROSE SERIES
BOOK 8.1

LOVE IN THE FORTRESS

COMPANION STORY TO
EMBRACE THE HUNT FEATURING
THE FAE-SLAVE, SANDRA

CARIS ROANE

Dear Reader,

Welcome to a special companion book called **LOVE IN THE FORTRESS**. In this book, you'll meet Sandra, the fae-slave from EMBRACE THE HUNT, who serves the villainous Ancient Fae in her castle-like fortress in the Dauphaire Mountains.

Sandra plays a critical role in EMBRACE THE HUNT when she delivers a key to the Ruby Fae that enables her to escape her imprisonment.

When Sandra first appeared, I had the sense she would make a great heroine and I was right!

With the help of Mastyr Vampire Griffin, a Guardsman also enslaved in Margetta's fortress, the pair work together to not only aid Regan in making her escape, but in the process of one night they discover that love can actually happen even in the worst of circumstances. Their only problem now is how to escape the wall of spelled mist that has kept the fortress and Margetta's army hidden from the rest of the Nine Realms for hundreds of years…

A Mastyr Vampire. A beautiful fae-slave. Trapped in a fortress. Can love bloom in the midst of a nightmare?

Mastyr Vampire Griffin hates his enslavement in Margetta's fortress. He sought death a thousand times because of it, but was denied when the Ancient Fae brought him back repeatedly, forcing him to train her evil army. When a beautiful fae-slave, Sandra, tells him to live, he begins to believe his life could have more meaning than a tortured existence in Margetta's hidden army camp. But will his growing love for Sandra put her at even greater risk?

Sandra has served the Ancient Fae as her slave for thirty years after an Invictus attack destroyed her family. Sent to work in Margetta's fortress, grief for the loss of her husband and young son have dominated her heart. When Mastyr Griffin arrives, however, she begins to see that love can exist even in the midst of a nightmare. But when she reaches out to the solitary mastyr vampire, the dangers of fortress life threaten her at every turn, especially when she discovers she's one of the most coveted women in the Nine Realms: a blood rose.

Enjoy!

Caris Roane

Chapter One

"Sandra, don't." Griffin held her arm in a gentle clasp, his voice low and insistent. "It's too dangerous. You've lasted this long. Why risk everything now?"

Sandra glanced up at him, at his intense light blue eyes, and her heart tightened in her chest. Sometimes the way he looked at her, like he did now, made her think the Goddess hadn't forgotten about her after all.

Griffin was always looking out for her.

But right now she had a job to do and meant to see it through.

She kept her voice to a whisper. "I have to do this. I have to help the Ruby Fae escape. It's my destiny. The reason I'm here. I'm convinced of it."

"There's no such thing as 'destiny'. Only survival. And I need you to survive. You've become important to me. Dammit, Sandra, don't do this."

She searched his eyes, stunned by his words. Was it possible he cared about her as much as she'd come to rely on him? He'd made the last year in the fortress a place of hope for her. Maybe she'd done the same for him.

He stood six-five in his traditional Guardsman black leather pants and incredibly sexy thigh boots. He had long hair like all the warriors who served Mastyr Ian of Camberlaune. Though since his capture, he'd lost the traditional woven clasp to hold it back. Instead, he used a piece of leather to keep his thick black hair in place.

Her heart responded as it always did to the warrior, like it had never known how to beat before. Or at least not for a long time, not since she'd come to the Ancient Fae's fortress thirty years ago.

And he was worried about her.

Still holding her arm, he glanced up and down the corridor.

She felt his nerves.

Hers were the same.

On fire.

She stood with him in the hallway by the fortress kitchen, her hands shaking. She was attempting to match the black wrought iron key she held in her hand to the duplicates hanging like laundry on a row of pegs down the corridor. If she could slip Mistress Regan a key, the woman could finally escape her tower cell and flee the fortress. At least, that was Sandra's current hope and plan.

Margetta had abducted Regan, also known as the Ruby Fae, from her Fae Guild retreat in Swanicott Realm a full month ago. The entire fortress and adjacent army camp had talked of little else since. Having Regan locked up in the fortress tower was a tremendous coup for Margetta. Rumors had flow that soon the Ancient Fae would put her massive army in motion and complete her takeover of the Nine Realms.

Sandra despised Margetta and her Invictus army more than anything. And the longer Regan had remained locked up, the more powerful Sandra's drive had become to do what she could, even to risk her life, to help the woman escape. The Ruby Fae had a wonderful reputation among all Realm-folk. She was known as a very wise, gifted fae who spent her years training lesser fae in their powers and in the ways of the Fae Guild.

Yes, Sandra believed it her destiny, something that might redeem her thirty years of dressing Margetta's hair, preparing her rose water baths, and trimming her disgusting toenails.

Griffin could argue with her all he wanted, but Sandra had to find the duplicate key.

She'd stolen the original from the fat troll guard who had command of a number of the fortress keys, including the one to the tower cell. She'd brought him a forbidden pint of fortress-brewed beer while he was on duty, knowing he'd soon be taking his tour of the dungeon cells. While he guzzled, she'd slipped behind him and taken the key from its hook. Before he could gather his senses, she'd offered to walk with him to the stairwell. He'd leered at her in his usual way, twirling the key ring on his finger.

As soon as she located the duplicate and matched it to the original, she would return the key to the guardroom. But it had to be soon, before the guard climbed the stairs and reached his station once more. If he discovered the tower key was missing, he'd sound the alarm, which is why she didn't want to give the original to Regan. Handing over the duplicate to the Ruby Fae would offer Sandra a layer of protection.

Griffin leaned close again. "And how do you propose getting the key to the Ruby Fae once you find it? Or have you forgotten you have company every time you head to the tower?" The same troll guard went with her, key in hand, to unlock the cell door. He was also known as one of Margetta's most loyal spies.

"That's the easy part. I'll roll it in a towel and take it with me for the next meal." One of her jobs was to carry meal trays to Regan's cell three times a night, a service she performed happily for the fortress housekeeper, Yvonne.

The good woman, a troll enslaved to Margetta for the past sixty years, was presently having a lie-down in her bedroom. She often stretched out on her bed between meal preparations, a brandy bottle clutched to her chest. At this hour, most of the house staff was outside gathering food for the next meal, combing the forest for deadfall for the camp fires, or doing the army staff's bidding.

Sandra, as one of three personal maids to the most wretched woman in all the Nine Realms, rarely left the stone walls of the fortress. She had recently finished dressing Margetta's blond hair in the long curls she preferred, which meant Sandra wouldn't be needed by her mistress for at least a couple of hours. So, if she was going to steal the duplicate key, now was the time.

Despite Griffin's disapproval of her plan, he stuck close as she checked key after key.

"I hear someone coming," he whispered. "We should get out of here."

At that, she had to smile, but kept her voice low. "With your vampire hearing, no doubt you just zoned in on the rats scuttling through the upstairs bedrooms."

He grunted. "You shouldn't be doing this. You realize if Margetta finds out, she'll have you tortured and killed."

Sandra repressed a sigh. In so many ways, she was dead already. She'd served in the stone, castle-like fortress for nearly three decades as a house slave. Only the last year, since Griffin arrived, had she begun to feel alive again. But they were both fortress slaves, so what good would it do to get too attached to him, or anyone for that matter?

The past rose up suddenly like a terrible wind. She blinked slowly, her mind caught on the memory of losing her husband and young son during an Invictus attack. All the images became a demanding horror show, like watching a movie she couldn't turn off. Her boy, only four, had clung to her, burying his face against her hip as an Invictus pair slaughtered her kind-hearted fae husband.

The child had been next. The wraith had taken him to the corner and feasted. In turn, the wraith's bonded vampire had shoved Sandra to the floor, pushed her legs wide, and done painful things to her. These she barely remembered because her gaze had been fixed on her son, on hearing his screams, on the tragedy of being unable to save what she loved most.

After her family had drifted so quickly and painfully to the afterlife, she was sure she would be next, had prayed for it. Instead, though bleeding badly, she'd been carted off to the fortress. Years later, she'd learned Margetta had ordered her abduction. She'd wanted Sandra in her service specifically because of her looks. The Ancient Fae loved having beautiful slaves tending her.

How lucky could a fae woman get?

How cursed she felt.

And still did, except for Griffin's warm, surprising presence in her nightmare existence.

As the memory rolled away and the here-and-now returned, she realized Griffin stood in front of her. He had both hands on her arms, shaking her gently. "Come back to me, Sandra."

When she blinked rapidly and his strong Guardsman features came into focus, she nodded. "I'm here."

Griffin was so handsome, with light blue eyes, a straight nose, and a tough warrior demeanor. He had a constant frown between his brows and a way of shifting his eyes that made her think of a hawk in constant search of prey. He'd fought in the Camberlaune Vampire Guard, alongside Mastyr Ian and his brothers-in-arms for over a century.

Now he was here, captured in a raid on the hamlet of Wayford a year ago and forced to serve as a sparring partner for the Invictus warriors. It was that or suffer endless torture since Margetta would never let him die.

After one of the torture sessions, Sandra had begged him to stop putting himself in harm's way and to live.

He'd shifted his thinking after that.

"Are you okay?" he asked.

"Yes." But her chest felt caved in.

When she saw the pit of concern between his brows, she reached up with her thumb and pressed the furrowed skin. "I'm sorry, Griffin. Sometimes, without warning, the memories return."

He knew the story. She'd only known Griffin a month when she'd told him what had happened to her family. "I loved them both so much. Henrik was a soulful, worthy man and had never harmed another Realm-person in his life. Sweet Goddess, I hurt, even after all this time."

As though it were the most natural thing in the world, he pulled her gently into his arms and held her. She was stunned that even in the middle of captivity, something so precious had happened to her.

She smelled his skin, the soap he used, the leather of his work vest. All seemed to combine in a rich, heady fragrance like a warm summer field, that set her mind reeling. Was it her imagination, or had his scent become something richer and deeper. Or maybe her affection for him had. She loved being with him and wished more than anything she'd come to know him in some place other than the Ancient Fae's fortress.

~ ~ ~

Without thinking, Griffin had drawn Sandra close, wanting to offer comfort. He didn't know what to make of the feelings he had for this woman, or that all he could think about was kissing her, touching her, taking her to bed.

Would she even be interested?

He wasn't kind or scholarly, like her husband. He was a warrior, brutish, and determined to keep her from making this terrible mistake.

She'd become important to him, critical to his survival.

He'd met her the first night of his captivity. He'd been in a holding pen with several frightened Realm-women. Opposite him were three beast-like shifters who'd tried to assault one of the female vampires.

The hell he'd let a rape happen on his watch. He'd fought the men, using every Guardsman skill he possessed. But they'd been powerful outcasts in the shifter world and had slowly beaten him down.

His face had been a mess, blood pouring from his nose and mouth, when Sandra had entered the filthy room. She'd carried a stack of towels in her arms and was a vision with her red hair, luminous green eyes, and creamy pale skin. She'd been like a light in a dark cave as she moved into the stone chamber.

He'd been hunched over at the time, hands on his knees and trying to catch his breath before he engaged in round two or maybe it was round ten. She'd stared at him for a long moment, then shifted to take in the women huddled together, several of them weeping.

She finally turned to face the shifters. "Margetta provides women for all the slave men, all of whom delight in servicing the physical needs of her prisoners. But she doesn't allow any of her female slaves to be violated against their will. I suggest you apologize to the women. Now."

She had an air of authority about her and no fear. These two things alone spoke to the shifters as significant. Their species valued the command of hierarchy above almost anything else. Sandra, as he'd come to know her later, had by her attitude alone, established herself as dominant.

The shifters had backed down at once and made their apologies.

What she'd done had made a profound impression on Griffin. But he believed he'd become fixed on her when she then turned toward him, her back to the shifters and met his swollen eyes. She'd offered him a soft smile. "Welcome to the fortress, Mastyr Griffin. Your service to Camberlaune is well known. If you need anything, you have but to ask, and that's my promise to you. I was also told by the housekeeper to add her blessing as well."

She'd then handed him a towel which he'd used to wipe his mouth. He'd pressed the same to his nose.

After a moment, he'd held her gaze. "I won't be staying long."

Proud words full of air.

But he hadn't known until his numerous failed escape attempts, just how powerful Margetta was. The Ancient Fae had been determined to keep him in her camp until she was ready to bond him to a female wraith. That day hadn't come yet, thank the Goddess.

Sandra had then nodded. "Do what you must. But if you can, please stay alive. Surviving honors those who have gone before."

He'd risen up from his catch-his-breath posture and stared hard at her as she ordered the women to follow her to the baths. His heart had gone with her in that moment, trailing after her, staying with her every hour of every night since his fucked up arrival in Margetta's camp.

Later, he'd learned that Sandra had shown up in the holding pen on purpose. She'd told him she'd somehow telepathically received an image of him battling the shifters so she'd come to intervene.

When it came to his camp duties as a sparring partner to the Invictus males, he'd refused to fight at first. But after weeks of torture, during which Margetta brought him back from the dead about twenty times, he'd finally surrendered to his fate. The best he could do was to hold back the tricks the Guardsmen employed to battle Invictus pairs. In this way, his actions weren't completely traitorous. But relying only on his fists, a limited portion of his battle energy, and the occasional axe and dagger had proved one helluva challenge. He got hurt often as well as injured to the point of death at least once a week.

He kept the camp healers busy.

On his escape attempts, he'd gone every possible direction intending to simply levitate out of the camp. More than once, he'd sensed that a pathway existed that could get him through Margetta's invisible spelled wall. But each time he tried, confusion would eventually take him to the ground, the Invictus guards would seize him, and he'd endure another round of body-and-mind breaking torture.

Sandra had made his time bearable for the past twelve months. She'd come to him repeatedly with her healing power. He didn't know how many times she'd helped the healers bring him back to life. Ultimately, she'd strengthened his will to live and he'd become more accepting of his fate.

She wore the long white linen gown denoting her position as a personal maid to the bitch from hell. Her beautiful red hair was braided off to the side, though she often wore it on a crown on top of her head. Her large green eyes sparkled with life, despite her enslavement. And when she smiled, he heard the angels sing.

But her skin, so creamy white, made her look fragile and tugged on his warrior instincts to protect her, despite how strong he knew her to be.

He had it bad.

He was as familiar with her history almost as well as his own. Over the past year, especially since he'd gained house privileges and had lived in a decent dungeon cell, he'd had hundreds of conversations with her. They shared one thing in particular in common; neither had any remaining kin in the Nine Realms. All his people, including his parents, were long dead as were Sandra's. She'd even lost a husband and son. He didn't know how she'd survived the horrific way her family had been taken from her.

He'd never known a woman like her before. She was fully fae, not the usual vampire female he went for. She had a tender heart combined with what he'd come to know as a will of granite. She'd survived because she believed it was the best way to show her love for those she'd been unable to save. She was an exceptional, worthy woman.

Every morning when he went to bed just before dawn, he begged the Goddess forgiveness for his treachery because of the sparring sessions, then prayed for his death.

Each evening, when he woke up still breathing, he sought out Sandra to make sure she was all right. He consoled himself with the thought that maybe he would find redemption if he could keep her safe.

But how safe could she be when she'd made a decision to help the tower prisoner escape?

Griffin hadn't actually seen Regan, the Ruby Fae, but all the slaves knew Margetta had succeeded in capturing one of the most powerful fae in all the Nine Realms. She was also planning on bonding her to a powerful male wraith. As an Invictus, Regan would then have more power than she'd ever experienced before. Unfortunately, she'd also have a broken personality with little concern for others and a zealous willingness to obey Margetta in all things.

Only recently, Regan had helped Zane of Swanicott defeat a large brigade of Invictus that Margetta had kept hidden in the eastern part of Mastyr Zane's Realm. The fortress slave-staff, as well as the army encampment on the border between Camberlaune and Tannisford Realms, had talked of nothing else for a full week, of the numbers lost, of the possibility Margetta could actually lose the war and her bid for the takeover of their world.

Of course, these fears were balanced heavily with the reality that Margetta held the Ruby Fae in her tower.

And this was the woman Sandra was intent on helping escape.

Griffin could admire Sandra's intention, but loathed it at the same time.

From the moment she'd told him of her plan to give Regan a duplicate key to her tower cell, his battle vibration had raced through his body, trying to figure out how to stop her. Or if he couldn't, then how to protect her.

He glanced in the direction of the doors leading outside. It wouldn't be long before one of the Invictus vampires would come looking for him. He'd probably be beaten for not showing up on time. But when Sandra had told him what she intended to do, he'd lagged behind, intent on making sure she came to no harm.

When at last she reached the sole remaining key in the hallway, he watched her shoulders sink. There wasn't a match after all. Thank the Goddess.

The relief he felt was a wave that washed over him, allowing him to breathe once more. "You've done what you could; now you can let this go."

But she turned toward him, her lips compressed, her green eyes darkening. She spoke in a low voice. "You don't understand, Griffin. I've already made the decision to do everything in my power to help Mistress Regan escape. And if I have to turn the entire fortress upside down in my hunt for the duplicate key, then that's what I'll do. Although, I have toyed with the idea of getting the guard drunk so he won't follow me to the tower. Then I'll let the Ruby Fae out myself. And now I have to put the key back before he returns."

She then turned and moved swiftly down the hall. He followed after her, his hands clenched into fists. The first plan to get the duplicate key to the Ruby Fae was bad enough. But this new one, to take the original to Regan, shrank his balls.

"Please, don't even think it." He whispered the words over her shoulder a she hurried toward the guard's room.

The troll, whose job it was to accompany Sandra to the tower cell, would be only too happy to expose her traitorous efforts to Margetta.

She reached the guardroom and he watched in relief as she slipped the key back on its hook. As she retraced her steps then turned up the hall, he could finally breathe.

She glanced at him. "Why do you look so mad?"

He drew her to a stop, turning her toward him. "I don't want you to do this, any of it. I don't want you to risk your life. If anything happened to you—"

He couldn't finish the rest of the sentence. Instead his mind, or maybe it was his heart, burned with a sudden realized truth. Somewhere, in the middle of this nightmare in Margetta's fortress, he'd fallen deeply in love with Sandra.

Her eyes were wide and unblinking as she stared back at him. He had hold of her arms again. He might have released her, might have taken a step back, but a long swooshing sound came from her lips. She then leaned up and kissed him.

She kissed him.

Sweet Goddess and all the elf lords burning in hell, nothing had felt better to him in his entire existence than Sandra's lips pressed to his.

He wrapped his arms around her, pressing her hard to his chest. When her lips parted, he slid his tongue into heaven.

He groaned at so much wet softness, the promise of what she had between her legs. He sank into her mouth, then offered a slow push-pull of his tongue to give her a taste of what he had to offer.

The sudden sound of laughter down the hall had her drawing back, but he didn't want the moment to end, couldn't let it.

He switched to telepathy, something he could do with Sandra because she possessed a strong ability to path. *I don't want to let you go.*

Griffin. Her hands were on his waist, squeezing.

Glancing around, he released her, caught her hand then pulled her swiftly down a short hall leading to a half dozen storage rooms. Her slippers made a soft rasp on the hard stone floor as she moved with him.

He opened the door to one of the fortress's large pantries then pulled her inside. Careful not to make a sound, he shut the door.

If he'd had any doubt about her interest in the brief, forbidden moment, he was reassured when she threw herself against him. She wrapped her arms around his neck and held on tight.

He turned her, pressing her up against the thick wood door, connecting his hips to hers. She was breathing hard as he kissed her again. She smelled like heaven, like a combination of herbs from the garden. He recognized one as rosemary, but the other he couldn't quite place. Sage, maybe. Her scent worked on him in a powerful way, causing his hips to arch into her.

She moaned in response, her body writhing beneath his. Her hunger matched his own. Drawing back, he petted her face with his hand, stroking her alabaster cheek with his thumb. His gaze took in her dilated pupils and the way she kept catching her breath.

He savored the full length of her body, the softness of her skin, and her delicate herbal scent.

His whole body vibrated with desire, his legs shaking with need. He'd never used the slave women who serviced the men; he'd never wanted to. What he wanted was this and he knew she could feel his arousal by the way her hips moved from side to side. He groaned, leaned in and settled his lips on hers once more.

He was kissing her at long last.

Fire and love combined.

Hunger.

He hadn't understood that his drive toward her, to be with her in the fortress, to look after her, had been so much more than a warrior's instinct.

He loved this woman, loved her with all his heart. And he wanted to bury himself between her legs.

The housekeeper's voice called from down the hall. "Sandra, where are you? I need my feet rubbed and you promised."

As he drew back, he had to laugh. "From this to tending a troll's warty feet."

Sandra shrugged, but she smiled. "Yvonne has been here longer than me by another thirty years and gives me plenty of freedom for this small service. Besides," her eyes took on a distant expression, "She's my friend, a fellow-slave, and she's kindness personified. So, yes, I'll go from the magic of being with you to tending her aching feet. She works long hours and has very limited self-healing ability."

He leaned his forehead against hers. "You have a good heart, Sandra."

"So do you." She caressed his face. "But, Griffin, I didn't know."

"What? What didn't you know?" He needed to hear her say the words.

"What we have between us. It's love, isn't it? Until now, this night, I thought it was friendship. Or maybe what I'm feeling is just some kind of fortress desperation."

He wanted to say 'No, it's love', but he feared saying the words out loud. Life in the fortress was a struggle. If Margetta or any of the Invictus servants knew how he felt about her, it could be used against them. "This is unwise."

He felt her body grow still. "You're right, it is."

He drew back meeting her saddened eyes. "I didn't mean to hurt you by saying that."

"You didn't. You just reminded me of our reality." She planted her hands on his chest then gently pushed him away. "I should go."

He stepped back a few feet, giving her space. He was still aroused and would need a minute to calm down. She pulled two linen towels off the shelf as well as a bar of soap.

With her hand on the door, she looked back at him over her shoulder. "You're not my type, you know. Not even a little. You're too handsome, too big, too strong, too much a warrior. Sweet Goddess, help me."

Though the room was dark, his vampire vision warmed up her features and he couldn't let her go thinking he was okay with her scheme. "I won't help you hunt for the key."

She looked up at him, her eyes glimmering with tears. "I'm not asking you to. I don't want you in any kind of danger because of what I'm doing. But you should head out to spar before you're found and punished." She opened the door and slipped through.

He heard her call to the housekeeper. "I'm here, Mistress. I have towels and soap. Let me fetch the hot water."

Griffin remained in one spot, fists on hips, his gaze pinned to the floor. If he was at all wise, he would forget about her.

Then he smiled. She thought him handsome, strong, and too much a warrior. Like hell he was forgetting anything.

After waiting several minutes, long after hearing Sandra's voice, as well as the housekeeper's, fade to nothing, he left the storage room.

Heading to the north-facing door near the guard's room, he passed into the fortress vegetable garden then trotted in the direction of the training camps. The night was dark, almost moonless and as in the storage room, his vision lit up the vista as though the sun shone.

His chest tightened at the sight of hundreds of rows of tents as far as the eye could see. Wraith's shrieked as they flew overhead. Margetta had found a way to harness the unruly Invictus pairs and shape them into a formidable army. Goddess help the combined Vampire Guards and Shifter Brigades of the Nine Realms, because the Ancient Fae's army was bigger than the ruling mastyrs had ever thought possible.

Chapter Two

Sandra took her time easing the pain in Yvonne's feet, as much by a soothing massage as by the healing she released into the woman's knobby toes and flattened arches. Afterward, the housekeeper prepped the tray for Sandra to take to the tower. When she wasn't waiting on Margetta directly, Sandra served the overburdened housekeeper in any way she needed, including taking meals to the Ruby Fae.

Once there, she found Mistress Regan sitting on the high window sill. The powerful fae often levitated to the otherwise inaccessible place to look out over the army grounds.

Sandra didn't speak with her since the troll could hear their conversation. He waited on the other side of the now locked door, peering into the room through the barred window. The troll reported everything to Margetta.

Sandra gripped the tray in both hands, waiting in a submissive pose with her neck bent forward slightly.

Mistress Regan wrapped her long gown tight to her legs as she made a slow descent, careful not to hit any of the furniture while coming down. The tower was not a large space, just really tall and impossible to escape except by the door.

Regan was a beautiful woman with light brown hair and dark eyes. She had strong cheekbones and a lovely straight nose. But her real beauty lay within. She had a spiritual calm that somehow made Sandra feel better just by entering the small round chamber.

Once Regan sat down at the table, Sandra laid out the silverware and food in the usual order, careful to obey Margetta's rules to the letter: bowl and plate first, then an embroidered cloth napkin, large spoon, and a small ceramic cup of blackberry wine. Even this would be reported.

Fortunately, Sandra had exceptional telepathic abilities and had been able to path with Regan from the beginning. But even in this she kept their exchanges brief. Lingering too long in the room because she was pathing with the Ruby Fae could alert the troll as well. She might despise the guard for the soulless creature he was, but he wasn't stupid. *Mistress, I wish you to know that I'm attempting to find the duplicate key to your room, since the guard would notice if the original was missing. Once I have it, I'll bring it with the next meal.*

Regan took Sandra's hand, a gesture hidden from the troll because Sandra's body blocked his view. *I wasn't sure it was something you could do, but I'm very grateful. I have the worst feeling Margetta is planning to bond me to a chosen mastyr soon.*

Sandra was surprised. *A mastyr? Not a wraith?*

Yes, I know it doesn't make sense, but that's what Margetta told me earlier when she visited my room. I believe I'm to be a reward for a mastyr who has aligned himself with her.

Sandra remained perfectly still. *I'm very sorry, Mistress. Although you must be right about the timing because gossip in the fortress has been rife. But I'm doing all I can to find the key for you.*

I'm more grateful than I can ever express.

It's the least I can do for you and for the war against this terrible woman.

She left shortly afterward, more determined than ever to discover the location of the duplicate.

She thought about reverting to her original get-the-guard-drunk scheme, but Griffin was right. She'd have no chance of survival afterward since all evidence of the Ruby Fae's escape would point to her. Somehow she had to locate the duplicate and sneak it to Regan during the last meal before dawn.

She spent the next hour searching through the various cupboards in the lowest levels of the fortress. If she was questioned, she planned to say she'd misplaced an entire box of Margetta's favorite rose petal sachets. But no one asked what she was doing and for that, she was grateful.

There were numerous storage rooms and pantries, but she had no luck, even in the dungeon areas. Every key had a duplicate but the only places where they were kept were on the pegs outside the kitchen or in the guard room. But the duplicate to the tower wasn't in either place which meant it had to be somewhere else. But where? She just hoped Margetta didn't have it in her possession. If she did, Sandra would have to change plans and probably go with her get-the-troll-drunk scheme, after all.

As she returned to the slaves' dining room to have her own bowl of soup, one of the maids, Trisha, intercepted her, dragging her into the hall near the bathrooms.

The young elven woman's eyes were wide. "Mistress Sandra, I'm so sorry, but Mastyr Griffin has been wounded while sparring. Badly. He's lost a lot of blood. The healers have called for you. They have orders to summon Margetta if he approaches death, but as you know, it goes badly for all of them if she's forced to leave her labors. Especially for Mastyr Griffin. Margetta will torture him if she has to bring him back from death again."

The world went entirely white, except for young Trisha's face. Her pointed ears twitched and tears bloomed in her dark brown eyes. "Mistress Sandra? Did you hear what I said?"

Sandra patted Trisha's shoulder, but she wasn't sure how to answer her. Was it only a couple of hours ago Griffin had kissed her? Sweet Goddess, she couldn't bear the thought of Griffin suffering one more night at the hands of the Ancient Fae.

When the room no longer spun, she met Trisha's gaze, choosing to ask the hardest question. "How close is he to succumbing?"

"Very. The healers were most adamant you should join them immediately. It was Mastyr Fulton who did this."

Griffin's feud with the vampire in charge of the sparring line was well-known. He despised Fulton more than even the Invictus pairs. From the time Griffin had been a captive in the camp, Fulton had tortured a number of slaves for the pleasure of it and several had died. Yet somehow Fulton had managed to dispose of the bodies without Margetta becoming aware of the murders. The Ancient Fae punished anyone who killed her slaves.

More often than not, when Griffin took mortal wounds, Fulton was the author.

With her heart pounding, she swallowed hard. "Where is he?"

"In the stables."

"Please tell Mistress Yvonne where I've gone."

"I will."

Sandra picked up her long skirts and ran as fast as she could. Griffin was the reason she'd started feeling more like herself, like maybe she would be okay, like she could do the impossible and help the Ruby Fae escape. She didn't want him to die. And the thought of how cruel Margetta could be when she had to use her healing power to bring any of her people back from the dead was an equal motivation to do her part.

She raced down the hall and out the north door leading through the fortress vegetable garden. She turned to the right and hurried along the path beside a row of tall hedges. A couple of Invictus wraiths streaked through the air, jeering as she ran, but she was safe from them. Margetta had strict rules about the slaves remaining unmolested. Any Invictus attempting to harm a slave would be killed.

Even the most maniacal wraiths had sufficient self-preservation instincts to restrain their killing urges.

The stables were two hundred yards from the house, a leftover from the era of horses. The stone out-building now housed several motorcycles and ATVs, imported from the States.

She didn't need to be told which room Griffin was in since a cluster of sparring warriors had gathered around the central door. They were all slaves captured at various times during Invictus raids from a number of the realms. Griffin, one of the most powerful mastyrs in the sparring line-up, was their unacknowledged leader.

She pushed through the group and found Griffin stretched out on a table. Eyes closed, he writhed from the pain of the wound and several men worked hard to keep him pinned in place. But they struggled because the mastyr was so physically strong.

His suffering pierced her heart.

Two fae healers, both men who had slaved at the fortress for even longer than she had, worked on him. Each had their hands poised above two severe abdominal cuts. Vibrations of healing energy pulsed within the room.

For a moment she stood transfixed, her gaze watching Griffin's blood drip from the table to the stone floor beneath. The color was red and so very real.

She'd seen many wounds over the years and occasionally assisted with the healing process. But her recently acknowledged feelings for Griffin threatened to overwhelm her.

She forced herself to draw a deep breath. "I'm here. Tell me what to do." The words left her mouth before she'd even formed the thought. Even with her knees feeling watery, she kept moving toward the table anyway.

One of the fae looked back at her. "Thank you for coming, Mistress. We know you value Mastyr Griffin and we need your help. Can you calm him? He's not in his right mind and we'll be able to help him better if he doesn't thrash so much."

"Of course."

She spent the next hour with her hands on top of Griffin's head, letting her power flow into his mind and ease his pain. The more relaxed his body became, even in his semi-conscious state, the swifter his cuts began to heal.

An hour wore on, then another. Progress, though slow, was steady, and gradually the wounds began to close.

When most of the healing was done, he slowly opened his eyes. He blinked several times as though trying to make sense of where he was. Leaning close, she spoke quietly to him. She explained that he'd been hurt during sparring and he was now in the stables.

He held her gaze, then pathed, *You came. Thank you.*

Her heart swelled as she looked down at him. Affection swirled through her. *Concentrate on your healing.*

Tell them you'll take me back to the fortress to feed me.

She stared at him for a moment. Did he really want her to feed him? But what surprised her more was how much she wanted to do exactly that.

She nodded, then addressed the lead healer. "As soon as Griffin can walk, I'll take him to the fortress and offer a vein. Would you agree this is the best course?"

"Yes, Mistress," the fae said. "Opening a vein for him would complete his healing."

The thought of giving her blood to Griffin, however, caused Sandra's skin to grow warm and her heart to beat harder still. She put a hand to her chest. She felt very full as though her body was already preparing to take care of him. She'd never done this before and wondered if it was normal, to feel a supply building when you were about to feed a vampire?

When Griffin was at last on his feet and felt strong enough to walk, she slid her arm around his waist. He still wore his leathers and thigh boots, but otherwise was bare-chested. Another wave of heat, full of forbidden desire, washed through her.

She thought about her time in the fortress and how much her life had improved since Griffin had come. A year ago, she'd been lonely. But his presence in her life had changed all that.

Certain ideas began to coalesce in her mind and she wondered if she had the courage to follow through. If caught, she would suffer at Margetta's hands, but she wasn't sure she cared right now.

The kiss seemed to have made her willing to take risks she'd never considered before. That, and the fact she was hunting down a key and planning a crime for which she could lose her life if caught.

As she thought about feeding Griffin, she knew exactly what she wanted to do. She just wasn't sure if he'd go along with it.

He pretended to lean on her as together they headed back to the fortress. *You know this is just an excuse for me to touch you. Do you think anyone really believes you're supporting me?*

Doesn't matter. I like your arm around my shoulders. So, I hear it was Fulton again.

Yes. Of course. And Margetta never punishes him so he feels free to do whatever he wants.

Fulton had command of the most powerful sparring men in the camp, including Griffin. Fulton made no secret of despising Griffin. The problem was, Fulton was a more powerful mastyr than Griffin, which meant he always had the upper hand in any contest.

Sandra knew Fulton would one day be bonded to a powerful female wraith and his abilities would allow him to defeat any ruling mastyr vampire. According to camp gossip, he wasn't yet Invictus because Margetta was still hunting for an extremely powerful wraith for him. In Griffin's opinion, Fulton, by nature was already Invictus. He enjoyed killing and took a psychopath's pleasure in torture. If ever bonded, Sandra knew he'd make a fully evil adversary.

If Griffin had been the more powerful mastyr, he would have been a threat to Fulton. But given his greater abilities, Fulton had happily taken Griffin to the point of death many times in the past.

Griffin cleared his throat, then spoke aloud. "You don't have to feed me."

Sandra grew very quiet, her thoughts tunneling inward. For a brief moment, she was back in the storage closet locked in his arms. She remembered the feel of his lips against hers, his body, every manly part of him.

"I want to feed you."

Griffin had always used the slaves Margetta provided for the vampires, when his blood needs grew demanding. As a mastyr, he had to feed every night. He suffered, as all mastyrs did, with a form of chronic blood starvation no mattered how often they used their fangs. Essentially, he was in pain all the time.

But as a mastyr, he was more powerful than any average vampire, one reason Margetta had wanted him to spar with her troops. He'd be the equal of any bonded Invictus male and more often than not superior to them. Sparring with him would make the Invictus warriors more effective in battle.

Sandra knew this part of Griffin's reality kept him in a guilt-ridden state. But she was also aware that he took pains not to demonstrate the most advanced skills he had as a Guardsman. In that way, he believed he protected his brothers-in-arms. It was also the reason he got wounded often during the one-on-one contests.

Arriving at the end of the hedge, he guided her to the left, back through the extensive fortress garden. His hand caressed her waist, then moved slowly down to linger on her hip. When he dug his fingers in just a little, she gasped softly. It felt so good.

He leaned close as he pathed, *Don't feel obligated to feed me. I can get one of the camp's doneuses to take care of me.*

She met his gaze, and forced him to stop for a moment. With no one else around, she planted her hands on his chest, then pathed, *I can't let you do that, Griffin. Right now, you're mine.*

I want to kiss you.

And I want you to do a lot more than that right now. In fact, I'm counting on it.

He held her gaze and she watched his eyes fall to half-mast. His summery field scent sharpened so that she felt kicked at the back of her knees.

Are you sure? he pathed.

Absolutely.

Where can we go?

I have a place in mind where we won't be disturbed.

She put them both back in motion, only she moved more quickly this time. With things settled, she was anxious to be alone with him.

Though she needed to find the duplicate key, right now she felt a strong urgency to feed Griffin. She wasn't sure why, but nothing seemed more important. And right now, her heart felt laden, like it had been waiting all this time to provide him sustenance.

Opening the door to the north fortress entrance, she headed swiftly down the hall for a few yards then took the servants' stairs to the right.

He followed after, but caught her hand a few steps up, forcing her to stop. *I'm not allowed up here.*

She smiled and tugged his hand. *You are just this once. Don't worry; Margetta adores me and if we're caught she'll forgive me. She knows I've never taken a lover and believe me she's suggested it about a thousand times.*

But it's the women's quarters.

It'll be all right. You'll see. Besides, at this hour, all the slaves are helping out in the camp. It's feeding time at the zoo, you know.

He chuckled at the slang term for keeping the Invictus army fed. She laughed with him. But once she reached the second floor, she levitated, moving swiftly down the long central hall.

He tracked with her, the powerful vampire that he was. *Nice moves, fae-woman.*

Thank you.

She took him straight to her bedroom, a small chamber housing a chest of drawers, a nightstand, and a double bed with an ornately carved oak headboard. Off to the left was her bathroom. On the windowsill was a vase of roses.

"You have flowers in here."

"I do." She closed the door quietly and turned the key in the lock, leaving it in the aperture. She couldn't believe she was doing this, that she was alone with Griffin, in her room, intent on taking him to bed.

~ ~ ~

For a long moment, Griffin stared at the flower arrangement sitting on the sill of Sandra's bedroom window. She'd kept a piece of civilization with her, despite her slavery. In some ways, the flowers represented who she was, her beauty, her velvety complexion, her strength.

"I should wash up," he said, suddenly aware he had blood spatter all over him from his wounds.

She crossed to the bathroom door and shoved it open. "One of the perks for being favored by the Ancient Fae. And please, take as long as you need."

There was a small shower in which he would barely fit. But after wrestling off his boots and leathers, he took his time scrubbing head to foot, even washing his hair. He'd fallen in the mud, letting the slide of his feet during the sparring session cover for his ongoing restraint.

He'd been battling Fulton, who loved to show off, and thought he'd bought it as he fell. Fulton had sliced him through his organs almost to the spine, in two different places. Part of him hoped to hell the healers wouldn't be able to fix him this time or Margetta, either. However, the healing team was well-motivated, death usually following the demise of any of their more important warriors. Margetta was unforgiving.

With the last of the dirt down the drain, he shut off the water and stepped into the equally small bathroom. He dried off, getting as much water from his hair as he could.

His thoughts strayed to Sandra, to how much he'd wanted this with her and for such a long. He would take it slow. She hadn't been with a man in years and she was probably really nervous.

Those thoughts, however, ramped him up instead of settling him down. His nostrils flared, because he would swear he could smell her soft herbal fragrance streaming into the bathroom, of rosemary and what he was now sure was sage.

Yeah, he was out of his mind for her.

But he also wanted to make this a good experience, so he worked at calming himself down.

He wrapped the towel around his waist and opened the door. He even had a speech prepared for how he knew this might be unsettling for her, since she hadn't been with a man in a long time.

Instead, his mind grew full of nothing. Sandra clearly had ideas of her own. The bedding was gone except for a couple of pillows. She lay on her side completely naked, her arm across her stomach which gave him an excellent view of her full breasts, peaked in the cool air.

She had a small thatch of red hair at the juncture of her thighs. Her creamy skin glowed against violet sheets.

He realized he was standing mute in the doorway when she held her arms out for him. He lost the towel, letting it fall to the floor. She'd already felt his arousal and had some idea what he looked like. She might as well see everything.

As he moved toward her, she lifted up on her elbow, her eyes flaring as her gaze fell to his chest, his abs, then lower to his groin. Seeing her had already started thickening him again.

"Oh," she whispered. Her lips moved, a sensual sight that had him wishing for things maybe he should keep to himself.

But she made a come-to-me gesture with her hands, quick flips of her fingers, so he slid onto the bed and got close, rising up on his knees. That's when he knew he was in real trouble. She had no inhibitions and as soon as his hips drew close, her hands were on him.

"Come closer and feed me," she whispered.

He was pretty sure his eyes rolled in his head. And they definitely did when he felt her tongue lick a loop around the crown of his cock.

He groaned heavily as she took him into her mouth.

She pathed, *We'll need to keep things quiet.*

"Right." He wasn't sure how easy that was going to be.

As she began to suck, she lifted her gaze to his and pathed, *I have a confession to make, Griffin. I've thought of you this way so many times with my lips surrounding your cock.*

Fantasies?

Yes, while I had my hands between my legs.

He stroked her hair, running his fingers down her braid. *I've been the same way. I've wanted you for months.* His hips arched into her and she took him deeper into her mouth.

When she sucked more aggressively, he restrained a moan. *You have no idea how much I've wanted this. Thank you, Sandra.*

My pleasure. Truly.

When he knew he was reaching a point-of-no-return, he pushed gently on her shoulders. *It feels too good.*

She released his cock, smiling, then rolled onto her back. She looked so beautiful, her body undulating, her nipples in tight beads. As he shifted to stretch out on top of her, she spread her legs for him. He kissed her, settling his hips between.

She moaned with pleasure, though keeping her voice quiet as her body moved beneath his. Her legs stroked his thighs; her hips arched.

He drew back enough to look into her eyes. *I'm so glad we're doing this.*

Me, too.

He reached down and took his cock in hand, guiding himself into her beautiful wetness. Her fresh rosemary-sage scent filled in the air. Did she wear a perfume, which seemed unlikely given none of the women had access to anything like cosmetics? Whatever it was, his desire for her sharpened because of the way she smelled. He loved it.

He began to push and with each roll of his hips, her body arched, drawing him deeper inside. Her hands worked his arms, squeezing his muscles so of course he flexed for her.

She gasped in response. Her parted lips were an invitation and he crashed down on her, kissing her again.

She wrapped her arms around his shoulders, her legs hugging his hips. He moved faster now, a steady rhythm that kept her moans flowing softly.

However, he felt an unfamiliar vibration deep within his body. *What is that?* she pathed.

He drew back, his hips slowing. *You can feel the vibration?*

Yes, and it has the most erotic and beautiful quality to it, as though it represents all that you are.

Her sudden intake of breath had him asking, *What? You know what it is, don't you?*

She nodded. *Griffin, I'm pretty sure it's your mating vibration. I can feel my own now as well.*

Of course. His mating vibration. He'd never accessed it before since he'd never had the kind of relationship with a woman where he'd wanted to engage in that way.

But with Sandra, it felt right and erotic as hell. *I want to touch yours. Will you allow it?*

~ ~ ~

Sandra didn't answer right away. They'd drifted suddenly and without warning into deep waters. Though she knew him well from all their conversations, their situation had hardly allowed for real dating. She didn't, therefore, know him at all on an intimate level. She'd been mate-bonded to her fae husband and it had been an incredibly beautiful experience, something many married couples chose to do.

So for Griffin to ask to touch her mating vibration was significant. Yet their situation was extraordinary, their relationship untried.

But as she looked into his blue eyes, always so intense, she knew she wanted nothing more. *Do it,* she pathed. *I want to feel you in this way, no matter what the future holds.*

Of course, exploring each other's vibrations wasn't a bond, just a sweet delight that could add to the pleasures of sex. Though, if they weren't careful, it could lead to an unexpected joining.

While his cock thrust in and out, she felt his mating vibration strengthen. By practice, she opened to him and his erotic frequency slipped inside her body, covering her own sensual waves of mating energy.

He started to groan, a rough sound that made her touch his lips with her fingers. "Shhh … "

He smiled. *Sorry. Couldn't help myself because this is unbelievable. So much more than I expected.*

It's wonderful. She lifted her hips slightly then curled her pelvis, something that helped her feel his cock as he drove deeper. It felt so good to be making love with him.

She closed her eyes, savoring the abundant sensations, not knowing how this much pleasure had suddenly come to her in Margetta's fortress.

Griffin, sex with you is magical.

He grunted quietly. *I feel the same way because I'm with you.*

When he pulled his long damp hair off to the side, she knew where he was headed, that she'd made a promise to feed him. His lips touched her cheek, gliding down to her throat. She'd never done this with a vampire before, offered up a vein in the middle of sex. But the idea of it sent her heartrate soaring.

When she felt his breath on her throat, her body clenched. *May I,* he asked.

Please. Yes. I long for it. Knowing she would feed him, she became aware of her heart and how it seemed almost heavy with nourishment. Was it because she loved him, as though her affection for him had translated into her heart aching to feed him?

He licked her throat above the vein, helping it to rise.

When his hips grew quiet, she knew his fangs had emerged. In anticipation of the strike, she clenched around his cock, deep inside her sex.

She felt his head lift up for a fraction of a second and the next moment he struck. Pleasure began to cascade in a series of shivers all down her neck and side and continued as he formed a seal with his lips and began to drink.

Sandra grew very still, not from fear or pain, but from the wonder of being so thoroughly pleasured at her throat, between her legs and the exquisite feel of his mating vibration stroking hers gently, all at the same time.

But when his hips began to move once more, the vibrations within her body deepened so that soon she was gasping for breath. A kind of euphoria had begun building around her heart. She'd never experienced anything like this in the entire course of her life.

Everything she'd felt for Griffin coalesced as he suckled. She admired his warrior mind and valued the way he protected those weaker than himself. But mostly, she treasured all the times he'd sought her out just to talk with her, to see how she was doing, to ask if she needed anything.

Still suckling, his hips moved into her faster now. She wrapped her arms tight around his shoulders. Her body was quickly rising to a place of release. *It won't be long for me,* she pathed. *I'm overcome.*

I love you, Sandra. Had he actually said those words? He had and she knew he meant them, as well.

Just as she did. She moaned but quickly bit back the sound. *I love you, too. So much.* Tears touched her eyes.

With his lips suckling her throat, he moved into her deeper still. His mating vibration made profound circling motions around her own, so that her vibration pulsed heavily, keeping pace with her sex.

She was breathing hard as she dug her nails into his back. *That feels good, Griffin.* She drifted her hands lower to his waist, then his buttocks, loving the rise and fall of his hips as he drove into her.

I love your fingers digging into me.

Griffin, she pathed, though no other words followed.

He must have understood her need because he began to thrust harder. Suddenly, he released his hold on her throat, swiping the wounds to seal them.

Lifting up, he locked his gaze with hers. She held his buttocks in her hands and slowly began to press her nails in.

Are you ready? He pathed.

She nodded.

And with his mating vibration moving swiftly and keeping time with his hips, ecstasy gathered like a mounting wave. Higher and higher it rose, taking her to the top and Griffin with her.

He slammed into her now, going vampire fast.

The wave peaked and pleasure became a powerful streak of lightning moving over her sex, and into her, up and up, pulsing rhythmically. She'd never felt anything like it as Griffin grunted his release, holding back the sounds she knew he wanted to make.

But on the pleasure flowed through her mating vibration as he stared at her. His neck arched, and she could see he was holding back, his teeth gritted. His pleasure matched hers and once again she rode straight to the top and plummeted over. She wanted to scream, but couldn't. Instead, she gripped his arms, his waist, his hips, his buttocks, her body writhing beneath his until at last the wave flowed to shore.

As her breathing began to settle, her body felt so light, her heart as well. She couldn't remember feeling this good in a long, long time.

His mating vibration still held hers fast, pulsing softly. It would take so little to complete the bond and for a powerful moment she wanted nothing more.

She took steady breaths as Griffin hovered above her, still connected. He was breathing hard, having done most of the work. His skin was flushed but a smile curved his lips.

He met her gaze. *I feel amazing. Really amazing. Different, somehow.*

She chuckled, keeping her laughter quiet. *How long since you last had sex?*

He looked thoughtful and his brows rose. "A week or so before I was captured. I'd been with one of my *doneuses.*"

She was sorry she'd asked because she felt a sudden powerful impulse to find the woman and scratch her eyes out. The sensation was so profound, even Griffin reacted to it. *What's wrong? Shouldn't I have answered your question?*

It's not that. For reasons I can't explain, I reacted with a fierce desire to hurt the woman. She laughed, thinking it was absurd.

At that, he relaxed on top of her. He was still connected and made no move to disengage. She loved it and took the opportunity to rub her hands up and down his arms. He was so built, so muscled. She took her time.

I love that it bothers you.

She shook her head. *I have no right to such thoughts.*

He glanced around, frowning. *And now I've had the worst thought, very unromantic, that I need to get back to sparring.*

She nodded. She hadn't forgotten everything about sex and withdrew a cloth from beneath one of the pillows. He saw it and smiled. *Good thinking.* She even loved his deep voice within her mind, a resonant sound that made her sigh.

She would have made use of the linen herself. Instead, he took it from her and gently performed the task while drawing out of her. It was incredibly thoughtful and her heart warmed up.

Thank you for this, Sandra. It was beautiful.

It really was. She smiled and repeated what she'd said earlier. "Magical."

He nodded, leaned down to kiss her once on the lips, then headed to the bathroom to clean up.

Sandra stayed where she was but drew the sheet up to cover herself. She needed Griffin to leave because they'd already risked so much being together in her room. But she feared if he saw her naked again, he'd want to stay.

She shifted her gaze to the roses on the windowsill and the twilight she saw because of her fae vision as she stared out at the night sky. The land sloped at this end of the fortress, so she had a view of the beauty of the Dauphaire mixed forest, the shapes of the bare trees and the dark green of the conifers. She loved all the seasons.

When Griffin returned, he was buttoning his leathers. His chest was bare, his thigh boots zipped up. He'd wiped them down as well. Normally he would have worn a vest, but it had been cut away from him when he'd been injured.

His gaze swept her sheet-covered body. "I'm grateful you did that, but was hoping for something else."

She smiled. "I know. That's why I covered up. I thought there was a good chance if I didn't, you'd never leave."

She watched his chest rise and fall. "You were right. I wouldn't have. I would have stayed."

She nodded, her head sliding on the pillow. "Come give me a kiss, then get out of here."

He drew close to the bed once more, dipped down then took his time, plucking at her lips and teasing her to open. She slid a hand beneath his long hair and caressed his neck. She parted for him and he plunged his tongue inside.

Her whole body seemed to rise up toward him, every muscle flexing, wanting to be closer.

I have to go. He drew back, his lips swollen, a glitter in his eye.

She looked away from him, feeling as though she was holding herself together with a delicate length of string. If he touched her again, or kissed her, or anything else, the string would break and she'd haul him back to bed.

Fortunately, he rose up then began walking backward to the door. "I love you, Sandra."

She nodded again. "I love you, too." Oh, sweet Goddess, so much more than she should.

With that, he turned on his heel, moved to the door then unlocked it.

"Levitate," she whispered. "No noise as you leave."

"Got it." He pulled the door open then closed it behind him.

He was gone.

Quick tears rose to her eyes. For some stupid reason she thought making love with him would ease her and perhaps physically it had. But now she craved him worse than ever.

She trembled as she rose.

Yvonne would need her soon and might be missing her presence in the kitchen already.

She hopped in the shower and made quick work of cleaning up. Dressed once more, she moved swiftly back to the kitchens.

~ ~ ~

"Took you long enough to feed." Mastyr vampire Fulton ran the sparring line. He was completely bald but had exotic red and black tattoos over his entire skull. His nose was broad and his black brows thick.

As mastyrs went, he was even more powerful than Griffin and would soon be bonded to an equally powerful wraith. Margetta favored him as one of her more loyal subjects.

Once he was Invictus bonded, he would gain substantial power, even more than Fulton presently possessed. He'd be able to defeat any of the ruling mastyrs, for one thing. And Fulton was the one who'd delivered the near-fatal slices of his dagger that sent Griffin to the stables for healing.

Griffin despised Fulton for many reasons, mostly his brutality. Griffin was convinced the mastyr had always been this kind of man. He was originally from Walvashorr, one of Mastyr Seth's Guardsmen and a significantly lesser mastyr than Seth. Griffin knew of more than one mastyr in the Nine Realms who would welcome a chance to have more power than any of the ruling mastyrs. Margetta's Invictus bond provided that means.

Rumors had it that Fulton had been promised a realm to rule once Margetta won the war. Griffin held his peace, but what motivation could Margetta possibly have to make good on any of her promises? By nature, the woman had no conscience.

Griffin thought Fulton was a power-hungry fool.

Fulton drew close to Griffin, scowling. "I wanted you dead. Thought this time I'd made the cuts deep enough."

"Guess you were wrong."

Fulton back-handed him across the face, throwing Griffin to the ground. The seasoned Invictus warriors around them showed no emotion. No one laughed or expressed pleasure that a Camberlaune Guardsman had gotten hurt. Fulton didn't tolerate any excessive displays. His men were well-trained by Fulton's tyranny.

Fulton sneered. "Get up, *mastyr*." His lips curled as he stared down at Griffin.

Griffin felt his muscles flood with power, more than usual, and his battle energy lit up like he'd never experienced before. His arms vibrated heavily, gathering a killing quantity. He rose slowly to his feet. He wanted nothing more than to lift his hand and release his power. But he didn't understand why he felt he could tear the more powerful mastyr to pieces right now.

Fulton faced him, his brows high, his dark eyes wild. A slow smiled curved his lips. "You want to kill me right now, don't you? I can see it in your face. Wasn't my dagger enough for you earlier? I can repeat it if you like. But this time, I'll sever your fucking spine."

Griffin didn't respond. He knew the moment he engaged in battle with Fulton, he wouldn't be able to stop.

Fulton's brows drew together suddenly. "Wait a minute. You think you can take me, don't you?"

That made Griffin stop in his tracks because Fulton was right. Not only that, Griffin knew it was true, he just didn't know why.

He watched Fulton's scowl deepen and knew the camp leader was processing new information. Griffin wanted to take him down, but if he did, how would he explain it to Margetta or anyone else? Especially, since he didn't know why.

Except that he'd fed from Sandra.

Holy shit.

He put a hand to his stomach, and on instinct looked back at the fortress. But that was a mistake, because Fulton threw a heavy punch, hitting Griffin square in the jaw. Griffin flew back into the dirt. He could have hopped up and fought back. Instead, he forced himself to stay put, feigning a knock-out.

He heard Fulton jeering at him once more, but apparently the successful blow had satisfied Fulton's rising doubts. He barked a series of orders for the sparring men to get back to business.

Griffin's mind whirled as he made a great show of struggling to get to his feet. Part of him was in agony that he couldn't go *mano-a-mano* with Fulton and send his sorry ass to the next life. But his greater commitment was to Sandra and if what he suspected was true, she was now in danger from every mastyr vampire in the camp.

Once on his feet, he lowered his head submissively and got back to work sparring with some of the more powerful Invictus shifters and vampires. But the whole time his mind was fixed on Sandra and wondering how the hell he was going to get a blood rose safely out of Margetta's fortress.

~~~

Chapter Three

"I've found a wraith to serve as your bond-mate. It's taken me a long time, Sandra, because I wanted a man of power for you, someone you could respect. He might be rough with you, but he'll rise quickly in the ranks, so it will be worth it."

Sandra's heart sank to her toes. "A wraith?" And a rough one at that? Oh, sweet Goddess, no.

She felt a flush of fear rising on her neck and flooding her face. The last thing she wanted was to become part of an Invictus pair. She would lose who she was and she'd become a killer.

Her knees felt wobbly.

Margetta stared at her in the mirror, her lips curving. "It's very odd. Your face went red, now it's white. Maybe you should sit down. I suppose I've given you a shock." She gestured for Sandra to sit on the button-tuck ottoman in the center of the Ancient Fae's large dressing area.

Uncertain her knees would hold her up, Sandra availed herself of the ottoman.

Margetta was preparing herself for her midnight meal, the one time of night she enjoyed a formal dinner with her husband,

Gustave. "But remember, once you're Invictus, you won't care about the comforts of fortress life, or the wraith's proclivities for bondage sex. You'll be content to be assigned tent quarters with your mate. And you'll finally get to have lots of sex on a regular basis. And you need it, honey, if you don't mind my saying."

Sandra had thoroughly enjoyed her marriage bed, but so much of the pleasure of sex for her was about being well-loved in all ways by a man she trusted. An ambitious, rough, male wraith? She felt sick to her stomach.

"Stop pouting. It will all work out. You'll see."

The Ancient Fae was a beautiful woman, with large violet eyes, well-shaped brows that Sandra plucked every other day, an elegant, straight nose and a softly pointed, fae chin. Her long blond hair hung in curls to her waist, also Sandra's work with the help of a super-heated curling iron.

She wore a floor-length gown of maroon velvet, matching heels, and a sapphire pendant. Sandra had just tucked a diamond-studded comb into the woman's hair, just off to the side, when the Ancient Fae had delivered her news.

Sandra had often marveled that what Margetta possessed abundantly in her physical beauty, she lacked to a corresponding degree in her soul. The woman was empty, completely devoid of decent realm feelings and compassion. If anything, she delighted in causing pain as she was now.

Uncertain what to do, Sandra swallowed hard. She was a slave and had to do her mistress's bidding or Margetta would have her killed. But to become Invictus? No, that wasn't acceptable on any level. She'd prefer death to a wraith-bond.

She schooled her features, however, since she didn't want the Ancient Fae to know her deepest feelings.

Margetta turned toward her, swiveling in her vanity table chair. "You look different somehow." She lifted her nose. "You smell sharper in your scent tonight as well. What's going on with you?"

Sandra knew better than to rise to the fly. The woman was fishing and the last thing Sandra wanted was to confess she'd taken Griffin into her bed. Margetta would demand all the details. Sharing with the Ancient Fae what Sandra had come to feel was one of the most significant and beautiful experiences of her life, was so not going to happen.

Sandra shrugged. "I've switched soaps. Maybe that's it. One of the undermaids gave me a bar with sage in it. Not sure if I like it." She wrinkled her nose for effect.

"Well that must be it. Now, what do you think of my news?" The Ancient Fae smiled. "You're to become part of my Invictus army at last and I think we'll have the ceremony just before dawn. How does that sound? In fact, I intend to preside over it myself."

"I don't know what to say." She really didn't. She wanted to tell the bitch to go to hell, but she also wanted to stay alive.

"Well, you mustn't think I have no feelings for you, Sandra. I do understand you'd rather not become a fighter, but we all must make sacrifices for the greater good. Wouldn't you agree?"

"Yes, Mistress."

"Your future bond-mate is a talented vigorous leader and together you'll accomplish much. You'll see. Now, I think a few of these curls need reworking." She turned back to face the mirror.

Sandra rose to her feet and moved to heat up the curling iron once more.

As she picked up the Ancient Fae's brush and began to perfect the two long errant curls that now fell from the diamond crusted comb, her thoughts turned to the Ruby Fae and to Griffin.

She had to come up with a new plan, because the last thing she'd ever do is join Margetta's army.

She'd die first. It was as simple as that.

~ ~ ~

At one in the morning, Griffin sat on the ground. Sweat streamed off his body from a couple of hours of intense sparring. He ate his middle-of-the-night meal made up of a tin plate of beans, sopping it up with a thick slice of bread. He had a mug of beer on the ground between his knees, protecting it. Rations in the camp were on the small side.

Margetta liked keeping her army hungry and sometimes a starving fighter would go searching for food to steal from a less powerful comrade.

It didn't happen often, because full-scale brawls often ensued and once again Margetta came down hard on the instigators, death always following. He had to give her credit for knowing how to keep her army in line. It also helped not having a conscience; she killed anyone she pleased, when and how she wanted.

As he took a swig of the beer, his thoughts turned once more to Sandra. With no pain in his gut, Griffin knew and understood the truth about her. The lovely fae woman was a blood rose, a powerful phenomenon making the rounds through the Nine Realms, a subject often discussed among the fortress slaves.

The latest news had been a really strange pairing between an outcast shifter named Olivia and Mastyr Zane of Swanicott Realm. Because they'd bonded, they'd been able to defeat Margetta's hidden army in Swanicott, which had happened a month ago.

He set his beer down unable to believe the impossible had happened because when Sandra had fed him, her enriched blood had ended his chronic blood starvation. He no longer had pain of any kind in his stomach and he'd lived with that pain since he'd become a mastyr eighty years ago.

He shuddered, however, thinking what would happen if by chance she encountered any of the camp's mastyr vampires. Gossip had it that the blood rose drive to feed a mastyr in need would be extended to all mastyrs until a bond was forged.

His gaze once more shifted to the fortress. He was only fifty feet away. He could get to her quickly if he needed to.

He knew her schedule extremely well. At this hour, she'd be sitting down to a meal for the household staff, though she'd likely have a nice soup with her bread, instead of a slopped out ladle of beans.

Griffin pictured Sandra moving around the kitchens, helping the housekeeper, laughing at some joke or other. He hadn't planned on taking her to bed, but it had happened. Goddess, he wanted to be with her again.

Fulton stood nearby, glaring at Griffin. The vampire's instincts had to be shaken up. He might not know exactly why he should be unsettled by Griffin, but he was right to be worried.

Yet in the same way Fulton was uneasy, Griffin kept his eye on Fulton. If the mastyr indicated in the smallest way he was going into the fortress, Griffin would be on his ass. The moment Fulton got near Sandra, he'd be all over her. He'd heard the gossip, but that wasn't how he knew what would happen. He could feel it in every bone of his body, the blood rose call on him, to get back to her, to be with her. And every mastyr would feel this way once they'd gotten close to Sandra.

As Griffin used his bread to clean up the last of the beans, he leaned his head back to stare up at the night sky. As he did, he began to see something he'd never noticed before, a strange mist high in the air hung over the entire camp.

Without having to be told, he knew he was seeing the actual physical structure of Margetta's spell, the one that had disguised the Ancient Fae's army from anyone passing nearby. He'd never seen the mist before. But he knew his ability to do so was another indication his recent engagement with Sandra had changed something in him forever.

Because he hadn't been paying attention to Fulton, the kick came out of nowhere, stunning him. Fulton made it a good one too, knocking Griffin's tin plate from his hands as his heavy boot landed on Griffin's jaw. He flew back several feet.

Griffin levitated swiftly in response and knew Fulton was winding up his battle energy. He felt his own rise in response. It hummed to the surface and flowed in waves down his arms, more powerful than Griffin had ever known before. Without a shred of doubt, Griffin knew he could kill Fulton right now if he wanted to.

But if he did, he jeopardized his own life as well as Sandra's. It was well known she'd fed him and his sudden increase in power would be talked about everywhere.

However, he couldn't keep taking Fulton's beatings, especially not tonight. He needed to be in top form.

As soon as Fulton released his battle energy from the palms of his hands, Griffin met that energy. His blue Guardsman power crashed into Fulton's red power, the color a sign that Fulton had given himself to Margetta and would soon have a wraith-mate.

A crowd gathered and wraiths flew above the battle, shrieking loudly. The shouting started, an Invictus roar that brought more and more of the wraith-pairs close to watch the fight.

But the moment he felt Fulton's power begin to thin, Griffin dialed his own down, matching him. He had to do his feigning act again, powering down in stages and acting like he was dead on his feet.

Once Fulton had drawn in his battling power, he came at Griffin with his fists. He let loose with a powerful right. Griffin took it hard on the chin, his head bobbing back. But he answered with a right hook then a low punch to Fulton's stomach.

Fulton doubled over. Griffin chopped the back of his neck and shoulders and Fulton fell to the grass. Griffin could have followed up with a series of painful kicks to his ribs, but instead knew he needed to pretend he was in a lot of pain from the blows Fulton had already delivered. He bent over at the waist and held a hand to his face. He sent healing energy to his jaw and his cheek.

Fulton was on his feet and leaped on Griffin's back, punching him in the side of the head. Griffin started spinning fast and threw Fulton onto several wraith-pairs. The crowd was hopped up, so they simply threw Fulton back in Griffin's direction.

Fulton levitated, catching his forward momentum and dropping down once more in front of Griffin.

The air however began to crackle, as a new entity arrived, one with more power than both vampires combined.

"What's the meaning of this?" Margetta's voice rolled over the crowd. Turning, Griffin saw that the Ancient Fae had arrived, looking dressed for a ball.

Silence fell hard and fast, along with a heavy dose of fear, and the crowd began to dissipate quickly. Margetta would be happy to punish the bystanders as well as those brawling.

With only Fulton and Griffin left, Margetta waved her hand back and forth between them. "What are you two doing? You're supposed to be training my army."

Fulton snorted. "Something's off with Griffin. He's not himself and I don't trust it."

Griffin had to play this smart. If Margetta figured it out, she'd make it impossible for him to get back to Sandra. Hell, she'd probably give Sandra to Fulton. A mastyr bonded to a blood rose, and under Margetta's control, would be a huge boon to her army, even more than if the mastyr was Invictus bound to a wraith.

Margetta drew near Griffin. He forced himself to stay calm, though he nearly lost it when she sniffed his skin. "You smell familiar to me. Like … " Her expression softened. "Well, well, well, you smell like sage, like a certain kind of soap one of the house slave uses."

He knew she was referring to Sandra. Sweet Goddess, the woman's scent was all over him.

Margetta smiled. "She told me she has a new soap. So what I'd like to know is how you happen to have her soap on you?"

The images of having made love to Sandra, and catching what he now knew to be her blood rose scent of rosemary and sage, rolled through his mind.

Would Margetta figure it out?

Goddess help Sandra if she did.

He decided to tell her a partial truth. "I fucked the woman, okay? I was in the fortress and it happened. She said she'd feed me after Fulton here gutted me earlier in the evening, and I took advantage of her. I wouldn't call it rape, exactly. But we were in her bedroom and I used her shower after the fact. She has a soap in there. Maybe that's what you're smelling."

At that, Margetta chortled. "Finally, the woman got laid. I knew she seemed different. I've been telling her for years to take a lover. Guess she was waiting for you. Of course you snuck one in under the wire; Sandra's going to be wraith-bonded just before dawn. I'm planning a special ceremony because she was always a favorite."

She turned toward Fulton. "And no more attacks on Griffin. I'll be getting you both bonded off to wraiths in the next couple of nights."

Because Griffin needed Margetta to leave, he spoke at the same time as Fulton. "Yes, Mistress."

Margetta levitated swiftly up to a balcony on the third floor where she had her private quarters with Gustave.

When she disappeared inside, Fulton grabbed Griffin by the throat. "This isn't finished. Margetta may have bought your bullshit, but I don't. Sandra doesn't sleep with anyone and if she did, she wouldn't choose your pansy-ass."

Fulton had been after her for a long time.

Griffin stared back at Fulton. If he had to, he'd kill Fulton. Right now, he let the mastyr huff and puff until he finally released Griffin and strolled back to the sparring lines.

Griffin stayed stuck in one place for a few more seconds. As his gaze again slid to the fortress, he knew one thing: He had to find a way to escape from the fortress with Sandra and he had to do it before Margetta forced an Invictus bond on Sandra.

~ ~ ~

The news that Margetta was planning a bonding ceremony within the next few hours, worked in Sandra's mind like a virus.

Each minute that passed filled her head with more and more of the Invictus horror. She knew what the pairs became, how changed the Realm-folk were once they'd entered the terrible bond. Each embraced battling with a maniacal fervor.

She didn't want to become that kind of woman.

She had few calm moments as she went about her post-midnight duties. Mostly, she stayed in the kitchen doing whatever Yvonne needed her to do. But her movements were agitated and more than once she dropped a pot or pan and finally shattered a glass bowl on the stone floor.

The housekeeper stopped her mid-stride and grabbed both her arms. She then yelled at her dish-scrubbers to get out.

Once she was alone with Sandra, she held her gaze and spoke quietly. "What's wrong? What's happened? Tell me, because I've never seen you like this before."

Sandra's voice caught on a sob. She didn't want to burden Yvonne, but she couldn't hold it in any longer. "I'm to be bonded in a few hours. Margetta has picked out a wraith for me."

The troll's three forehead ridges tightened. "Oh, no. I've feared this night would come and with the war heating up I'm not surprised. But my sweet Sandra, no. No, no, no, no."

Sandra was considerably taller than the troll, who squeezed both her arms tight.

Yvonne then released her and looked around. "Stay put. I'll be right back."

She left the kitchen and when she returned, she had a stool in her hands. Setting it on the floor near Sandra, she waved her forward. "Help me up here."

Sandra held the troll's hand as she assisted her in climbing up on the stool, though Sandra had no idea why she wanted it in the middle of the kitchen and not even close to one of the cupboards.

But when she was standing on it and facing Sandra, she gestured for Sandra to come close.

In this position, Sandra actually met the troll's gaze eye-to-eye. "What is it?"

"Sandra, you've been as dear to me as my own daughter, Eva. And I would do anything I could to keep this from happening to you. I'm so sorry. Now come here."

When the housekeeper opened her arms, Sandra finally understood. She practically fell on the woman and had to work to keep the troll balanced on the stool. But when Yvonne was steady, she held Sandra close, wrapping her up in her short, troll arms, the hug exactly what Sandra needed.

Nothing had felt better to her in a long, long time.

Except being with Griffin.

But how was she to keep the bonding nightmare from happening?

When Yvonne released her, Sandra helped her get down from the stool, returning it herself to the nearest pantry. While there, she remained smelling the unique food-stuff redolence, a sort of combination of flours, dried beans, and cookies in canisters.

For some reason, the scent calmed her and she could think. Yvonne's comforting embrace had helped as well to settle her mind.

Her thoughts turned to the war and to all the slaves who'd died in the fortress over the decades. She'd grieved for every death and each time promised herself that if she ever had the chance to make a difference she would take it, no matter the consequences.

An otherworld serenity came over Sandra, an acceptance that she might not survive the night. Somehow, that acceptance began to shape itself into a profound resolution to do whatever she had to do to assist Regan in leaving the Ancient Fae's fortress, even if it meant stealing the guard's key to the tower cell.

She closed her eyes and after bidding wisdom from the Goddess, she held her hands palms up and let her mind flow in ways it perhaps never had before.

She'd felt different since the lovemaking with Griffin, though until this moment she hadn't thought to analyze it. For one thing, despite the fact that she'd fed Griffin, her heart felt oddly laden again, as though …

Her eyes widened and she put a hand to her chest. She felt it now, a heaviness that wasn't emotional at all, but rather very physical. Something a blood rose would experience.

She gasped. She'd heard all the rumors, especially the latest ones about the shifter Olivia, who was now mate-bonded to Mastyr Zane. They'd become a Nine Realms power couple and all because Olivia was a blood rose.

Sandra didn't spend even a few seconds denying what she knew in the depths of her spirit to be true. She was a blood rose.

She was building a fresh supply even as she stood in the pantry, only it didn't feel Griffin-specific. Instead, all she had to do was think of the several unbonded mastyr vampires roaming the camp and waiting for wraiths with which to mate, and a profound need to feed each and every one of them rose within her.

When she found herself turning toward the door, ready to head out to find these vampires, she forced herself to hold only Griffin within her mind. She'd heard of this, as well. So long as she remained an unbonded blood rose, she'd crave every mastyr she came into contact with.

Oh, dear sweet Goddess.

As she focused on Griffin, she felt something rise within her, so powerful, like a geyser within her heart, that for a moment she couldn't breathe. It was as though the new sensations she was experiencing, the need to offer sustenance to a mastyr vampire, became exponentially enhanced when she thought of Griffin.

The reason had to be simple; she'd made love with him. But was it something more? Something that came from her heart?

She knew the truth again without wasting time denying what she felt. Her love for Griffin enhanced what she felt as a blood rose. She'd probably been in love with him from the moment she'd entered that holding pen a year ago and found him defending the newly enslaved women against three powerful shifters. He was a man who would go the distance, who would die trying to protect those he loved, and who probably had already guessed what Sandra had so recently become.

She trembled now from excitement and hope and from the love she felt for the vampire.

The next moment, however, she shaded her eyes and tears bloomed. The reality of fortress life, the spies who roamed the halls for Margetta, and that Griffin was required to be outside sparring until dawn, all worked against them.

But if something didn't happen in the next few hours, Margetta would force the wraith-bond on her and there would be nothing she could do to escape it.

Whatever she chose to do, she had to be swift and she had to be careful.

First, she decided to path Griffin, to see if she even could at such a distance. She'd never done so before, but she was a blood rose now and her powers had increased. *Griffin, are you there? I'm in trouble.*

When she didn't hear a response she tried again. And again.

~ ~ ~

Griffin sparred with a powerful shifter, mate-bonded with a wraith who floated above them shrieking the whole time. He used his battle energy in bursts and an axe in his left hand.

The shifter had once served in the Swanicott Shifter Brigade when he'd left to join Margetta's forces and engage in the Invictus bond. But he was no match for Griffin.

As Griffin levitated with sudden speed, and sent a minute amount of his battle vibration straight into the shifter's head, the shifter crumpled to the dirt.

Griffin was barely winded, but he feigned what his usual response would be and bent over at the knees, waiting with axe in hand for the shifter to revive.

Griffin, are you there?

The words were faint but unmistakable now that he wasn't fighting. *Sandra?*

Thank the Goddess you can hear me. I'm in trouble. I'm a blood rose, but I'm guessing you know that by now.

I do. He remained where he was and watched as the shifter slowly began to regain consciousness. Buying a little more time, he sent another blast and hit him in the chest. He rolled on his back, limp. *Tell me everything.*

He listened as she spoke of the new supply she was building for him, then a string of panicky words about needing to feed all the mastyrs in the camp.

At that, he tossed the axe onto the nearby weapons pile, rose up and moved in a circle. He shoved his hands through his long hair, dislodging the leather strap. He re-tied it.

But the thought of Sandra feeding even a lesser mastyr had his fangs vibrating heavily in his gums. He'd heard about the almost caveman-like visceral response to the blood rose, a drive to possess her and keep her away from all others.

There's more. Margetta intends to bond me to a wraith near dawn.

Margetta had already told him and he'd been struggling to create a plan to get them both out of the fortress within the next few hours. Nothing had come to him and maybe that's the reason he lost it. But he suddenly cursed long and loud, then roared into the night. He shouted every foul word that would come to mind.

Only when he stopped, he realized the entire sparring line now stared at him, including Fulton who was levitating in his direction.

Fulton. A mastyr vampire.

I'm coming to you. Somehow. Now. But I've got deal with Fulton.

He had to think fast, to get the hell out of there without tangling with Fulton. But how?

Then he knew what to do, the one thing that would make sense to every vampire in the sparring line, including Fulton.

"I need to feed," he shouted. "Now." Without one more word of explanation, he bolted toward the female slaves' quarters, those women who serviced the men with sex as well as the vampires from their veins.

When he was out of eyesight, he slowed but retained his direction. He had to think. How was he to get into the fortress at this hour? Yet getting there seemed more critical than anything else he'd experienced in the past year. He had to get back to Sandra and he had to bond with her. And it had to be now.

The lay-out of the fortress came to mind. The central entrance, though at a distance from the kitchen, was sheltered by tall hedges surrounding a large, rose garden and an expansive lawn. In that respect it was completely hidden from the army camp.

He made the decision, because it seemed the only way to get into the fortress with the least amount of eyes on him. He levitated swiftly and as soon as he saw the breach in the hedge that indicated the entrance to the garden, he slipped through, then flew to the carved double doors of the main entrance.

He pulled them wide and walked in.

Sandra, I'm in the entrance hall. I need you to come to me now. We've got to figure this out.

I'll be right there.

He drew deep breaths. He was filthy from sparring and this part of the fortress was full of marble and silk. Even his boots were dirty.

He heard running footsteps, light quick swishes on the stone then the marble floor. Sandra was forty feet away when he caught sight of her at the end of the long hall. She began running in earnest, levitating at the end.

His throat tightened as he headed in her direction, skirting a table with a tall flower arrangement to finally catch her up in his arms. She didn't seem to care that he was sweaty and once more covered in mud or that all the grime would no doubt end up on her white gown.

She kissed him as though her life depended on it and he returned the favor.

Back to my room, Griffin, now. You have to bond with me. You have to.

I want nothing more.

She drew back just enough to look at him. *Carry me and levitate. If you go fast, we can avoid the next shift of maids who will be heading up here in about two minutes.*

He didn't need another command. He held her tight against him and flew faster than ever, straight up the servants' stairs, along the hall and back to her bedroom.

Once inside, she locked the door again. When he stepped away from her he was appalled. "I got your gown dirty."

"I don't care."

He looked at his arms, at the recent sparring bruises, at the still healing cuts, at the streaks of mud, and he didn't want to think about what he smelled like. "I'm taking a shower."

Her smile was crooked. "Then I'll help."

At that, his lips curved. "You can't fit in there with me. The shower's barely big enough for me as it is."

"I know that. But I can stand nearby and soap things up. Big things."

He groaned. They were playing with fire, because if either of them was caught … He wouldn't think about that.

Instead, he moved into the bathroom and got rid of his boots, then his leathers. He'd been given a vest to wear and stripped that off next.

He heard an odd sound coming from Sandra. Turning toward, her, she had her hand to her mouth and her eyes were wide. Her gaze was on his ass.

He smiled again. He knew the effect a powerful male body had on women. Every damn muscle was a promise of good things to come.

He didn't close the curtain, despite that the floor would get wet. He turned the spray on and washed his hair. His whole body was flushed with need so he kept the water on the cold side. Even then, his cock was rigid and refused to settle down. Although it didn't help when she stripped off her own gown, bra and panties, then drew close and took the soap in her hands.

She washed his cock with care and a sensual touch that had him groaning. She shook her head at him. *No noises.* She then stroked him with both hands while she leaned up and kissed him.

He'd made love to her earlier but his drive toward her was like nothing he'd known before. His whole body became a vibration of energy and need. He felt his mating vibration hum within his chest.

I need you in bed.

She let her hands fall away then lifted them to the spray of water. She nodded, then dried her hands and moved slowly toward the door.

Once there, she stayed put for a moment, her gaze sliding down his body. She put her hands on her breasts and massaged both of them, her lips parting.

His cock jerked once, letting him know he needed to move things along. He cleaned up as best he could, left the shower and toweled dry. By then she'd moved back to the bed.

Only this time, she sat at the edge of the mattress, her legs spread and one hand moving slowly in the direction of the thatch of red hair between her legs.

He was hard as a rock as he moved toward the bed, his hand on his heavy cock, supporting himself as he walked.

Once he reached her, he pushed her back on the bed, then dropped to his knees. Lifting her legs to settle them on his shoulders, he said, "Allow me."

He had to shush the moan that came from her throat.

The moment he settled his tongue against her sex and her body writhed, he pathed, *You taste like rosemary and sage and I can't get enough.*

Chapter Four

Sandra lay panting. She'd forgotten how intense sex could be with a man she loved, though the experience with Griffin had definitely been enhanced because she was a blood rose.

Your tongue, Griffin. So much pleasure.

Good. Now look at me.

She lifted up on her elbows and met his gaze. His light blue eyes glinted as he laved her folds and teased her with flicks of his tongue. She gasped at each sensual touch.

Then he moved lower so that his tongue touched her entrance. Small light gasps left her throat. When he pushed inside, her whole body arched. The pleasure was incredible.

But to her surprise, suddenly she felt a vibration begin where he licked her. *Is that your tongue?*

Oh, yeah. His eyes were at half- mast.

She'd heard of this but she'd never experienced it before.

Her body trembled as the vibration increased and Griffin began to thrust at the same time. He went faster and all her need sharpened.

She put her hand over her mouth. *Griffin! Sweet Goddess!*

Want more?

You'll make me come.

Then come. He revved up the vibrations to an even faster frequency which sent her flying over the edge. She groaned against the palm of her hand, her hips jerking up and down. He held her tight with his hands on her buttocks and continued to plunge into her sex until the wave passed.

Her arms fell wide. She was breathing hard and couldn't keep her eyes open. *That was amazing.*

She felt him rise and slide an arm beneath the center of her back. She opened her eyes, meeting his gaze with a questioning lift of her brows.

He smiled. "I'm going to move you. I need you in a different position."

An excited shiver raced over her entire body.

~ ~ ~

With one arm, Griffin lifted Sandra, sliding her to the center of the bed. Her rosemary and sage scent was doing something to him and he needed to get inside her. His mating vibration pulsed heavily in his chest as well.

The vibrations he'd used with his tongue had been easily come by because his whole body seemed to pulse in a steady frequency. Above all else, he felt a profound need to please Sandra. He was a mastyr after his blood rose, wanting to be connected to her on every possible level and determined to make her his own so that no other mastyr could get to her.

As he settled himself between her legs, Griffin stared down at her. He felt in this moment as though his entire life came together.

He'd always believed in the divine purpose of things, that the Goddess in her wisdom brought forces together to bring about a better world for all Realm-folk.

For him, finding Sandra in this desolate place had been the divine purpose in his life. He hadn't had these thoughts at first, but they lived like fire in him now. She believed her own unique purpose was to get a key to the Ruby Fae so she could make her escape. Despite his fear for Sandra, he understood her drive to help Regan since in a similar way he now believed his job was to protect Sandra. Ever since he'd realized she was a blood rose, he'd become fixed on the idea of somehow taking Sandra out of the nightmare she'd lived in for the past thirty years.

"I love you, Sandra. I think I have from the first moment I looked into your green eyes." He stroked her hair, pushing some of the strands away from her cheek. He leaned down and kissed the spot, then trailed a bunch more all the way to her ear.

He French-kissed deep, sliding his tongue into her beautifully pointed ears, then licked to the sensitive tip. When he drew the point into his mouth and sucked gently, her whole body undulated beneath him. At the same time, she grabbed his arm and sunk her nails.

Everything you to do to me, Griffin ... unbelievable.

For fun, he added a vibration to the suckling, and a squeal left her mouth. He quickly covered her lips with his fingers. But her tongue made an appearance, licking each one until he had to put two of them in her mouth.

She suckled greedily, the way he wanted her mouth on his cock. She drew back, pushing him onto his back. "I need a taste."

He knew what she meant to do and he withheld a moan. As she moved down his body, he felt her hair brushing over his abdomen then her lips and finally her mouth as she took him inside. His jaw trembled and his breathing grew rough.

She held the base of his cock in her hand. *I don't know if I can add a vibration, but I'm going to try. Being a blood rose seems to have enhanced everything for me. Now let's see if I can return the favor.*

His entire body went very still when the first vibration rolled through her mouth. He couldn't breathe. Now he understood why she'd come so quickly. *Oh, sweet Goddess, that feels good. Too good.*

She rubbed his abdomen at the same time with both hands, gliding them down his hips and onto his thighs. She kept suckling though very gently and at the same time let the vibration flow over his cock. He wouldn't be able to handle too much, but she was doing it just right. If she'd sucked in earnest he would have lost it.

Instead, every touch of her hands, lick of her tongue, and wave of vibration ramped him up but didn't take him all the way. It was perfect.

When he felt his balls tighten, however, he pushed her shoulders gently. She released his cock then rolled once more onto her back. "Where were we before we got so beautifully side-tracked?"

He smiled at her words then moved once more between her legs. The moment she drew her knees up, he pressed his cock against her wetness. His breath caught.

He slid inside in one long drive that had her hips arching and her mouth opening wide. *Cover my mouth with your hand, Griffin. Please.*

He understood why. And the moment he did, she groaned against his palm. *It helps,* she pathed.

I know.

He began to rock into her, savoring the feel of her body writhing beneath his, as well as the way she gripped his cock with her sex. Moving faster, he kissed her cheek at the same time, loving the feel of her groans against his palm.

Griffin?

Yes?

Will you bite me?

He shuddered with pleasure and almost came. He had to stop for a moment and calm the hell down.

She panted lightly against his hand but didn't say anything. He knew she understood. He could sense they were in sync.

When he began to move his hips again, her tongue teased the palm of his hand. He smiled as he kissed a line down her neck. She angled for him and a soft cry of pleasure left her throat.

He took his time though, licking above her vein and feeling it rise for him. He was breathing hard now as he tilted his head. With his fangs descended and ready, he struck and her blood flowed.

He groaned as an elixir, laced with the flavor of rosemary and sage, hit his mouth, his tongue, then trickled like the most beautiful fire down his throat. He formed a seal around the wounds and began to suck. He lost a sense of time and place. All he felt was his cock driving into her once more, her body moving in heavy waves beneath his, and the amplified nature of her blood powering him once more.

He went faster, a strong dedicated rhythm.

Griffin. I love you.

His heart swelled and his mating vibration began to pulse, a demanding frequency that called to her.

Do you want this, Sandra? To bond with me? Are you sure?

Absolutely. I love and admire you and I value how you treat me, how you've been with me for the last year. I want to bond with you as your blood rose.

He grunted in response and the moment she opened up her mating vibration, he let his fly. His pulsing frequency swept over hers, teasing her with another layer of pleasure as it swirled back and forth in a rhythm that matched his hips. *It's coming.*

I can feel it. Oh, Griffin. She was gasping now, quick, harsh breaths against his hand.

He released her neck, swiping his tongue to seal the wounds. He lifted up enough to plant his right forearm beside her to give himself leverage as he thrust into her. But he also wanted to look at her as this enormous thing happened between them.

Her eyes were wild and shimmered with tears. Her body rolled with his. They were one heavy flow of joined sensation. *I bond myself to you, Sandra of Camberlaune Realm. I give myself to you as a husband, to serve and adore you the rest of my life.* His mating vibration began to tighten. *I love you, Sandra.*

And I offer myself to you, Mastyr Griffin of Camberlaune Realm, to be your blood rose, your bonded mate, your wife. I hold nothing back, but give of myself freely, loving you with all my heart.

With that, his mating vibration tightened completely, surrounding hers and merging to create one powerful shared vibration.

Sandra's eyes widened and a flush flew up her cheeks. She cried out against his hand as ecstasy took hold of her. He drove into her hard, his own body beginning to release. *Cover my mouth as well, Sandra.*

She pressed her hand tight to his lips. And as the orgasm began to come he grunted heavily, wanting to roar with the exquisite nature of every sensation, but he held back to protect them both.

Pleasure flowed from their joined mating vibrations, flooding his abdomen as his cock pulsed with fiery pleasure.

But this time the orgasm didn't stop. Instead, just as he was winding down, another series of pulses began to erupt from him.

At the same time, Sandra screamed against his hand, the pulses of her well pulling on him. He drove fast, wanting to make her pleasure last. Then, without warning, a sudden explosion of ecstasy erupted from their shared mating vibrations. His back arched and he had the devil of a time not roaring out loud.

And the blood rose bond locked into place.

He dipped his head back in her direction and met her astonished gaze once more. He slid his fingers off her mouth and she did the same, drawing her palm away from his face. He followed his first impulse and kissed her. She responded in kind, wrapping her arms around his shoulders and kissing him back.

After a moment, he met her gaze. "I can feel you, what you're experiencing, everything."

"Same here, especially the pleasure you feel with your cock inside me."

His lips curved. "And how much you enjoy my cock."

Tears formed in her eyes. He kissed her again and again. He didn't leave her body for a long time, but stayed connected to her. She was his woman now.

~ ~ ~

Sandra slid her hands around Griffin's neck, beneath his long, damp hair, then caressed his shoulders and arms. Her breathing had finally settled down. It seemed so strange to be back in bed with him, and even more bizarre to feel the way their mating vibrations had locked into place.

She closed her eyes and her fae senses came alive as never before. She felt the future floating around her like scattered images she could pull together to create a whole picture. She knew some of the fae of the Nine Realms had extraordinary powers and were able to experience visions of the future.

Until this moment, her own gifts had been very limited. Occasionally, she would experience a strong prescience about what was going to happen in a given situation. Yet right now she felt as though she could know things about the immediate future if she extended her fae power and put her mind to it.

But she didn't want to know. If she saw herself bonded to an Invictus wraith, she'd fall apart. Or if she saw that her relationship with Griffin had been discovered, she knew Griffin's execution would follow. Or hers. The burden of knowing would be too much to bear.

For now, she held the future at arm's length, savoring each stolen minute she had with Griffin in her bed.

Time began to drift by. Eventually, Griffin drew out of her, leaving her feeling strangely empty. He once more tucked a cloth between her legs and headed to the bathroom. She turned on her side a hand beneath her cheek. She needed to figure out what to do next, but felt horribly overwhelmed by the knowledge Margetta was planning her wraith-bonding ceremony in only a couple of hours. And she still needed to get the key to the Ruby Fae.

A knock on the door had her rising swiftly and putting on her robe. "Who is it?"

"Yvonne." The housekeeper scratched on the door. "Your absence has everyone talking. And Mastyr Griffin cannot be found."

She opened the door and met the troll's worried gaze. Sandra wanted to know what the troll would see, if Sandra looked any different now that she'd bonded with a mastyr. "I've not been myself tonight, so I've been resting. As for Mastyr Griffin, he probably went into the forest to hunt for deadfall." It was a stretch. To her knowledge, Griffin had only served on a couple of the wood-collecting forays.

Yvonne shook her head. "Fulton's been threatening to form a search party to look through every room of the fortress. I told him to shove off. He wasn't too pleased by my attitude, but these stone walls are my domain and the hell I will let him or any other bully invade my kingdom.

"But you would do well to return to the kitchen. Besides, I'll have the Ruby fae's meal ready in half an hour. Will you take it to her?"

Sandra gasped. "What time is it?"

"Almost half-four."

She put a hand to her lips. "Oh, Goddess."

But her fae powers intruded and this time the future rolled through her mind. She had a sense she was being presented with one possible path, not necessarily a fixed sequence of events, so she allowed the various images to come together.

A swell of pure excitement flowed through her, sending shivers racing over her shoulders and sides. She knew then exactly what she wanted to do and it included the fortress housekeeper.

She grabbed Yvonne's hand and pulled her into the room, closing the door behind her.

"What are you doing?"

"I have Griffin with me, here in my bedroom."

"What?" Yvonne looked genuinely shocked and all three forehead ridges drew so tight together the seams turned white from the pressure.

"Griffin. Come here."

The bathroom door opened and Griffin appeared on the threshold. He'd donned his clothes once more, though it appeared he'd brushed some of the dirt off.

"Look who's here," Sandra murmured.

A smile softened his features. "Mistress Yvonne. The miracle worker of the fortress kitchen. The meals you serve have made my life bearable, and I thank you." Those allowed to sleep in the fortress also had table privileges for the first meal of the night. The food was outstanding and Yvonne was the reason.

Sandra took Yvonne's hand then waved for Griffin to join her and take Sandra's free hand.

He frowned slightly "What's going on?"

"I've come to a decision. You both know Margetta intends to mate me to a wraith tonight and I can't do it. Won't do it." She narrowed her gaze at Griffin. "In fact, I'm not even sure it's possible at this point."

Yvonne's eyes widened and a gasp followed. "By all the angels serving the Goddess in heaven, you've bonded with Mastyr Griffin. I can feel it in these powerful vibrations flowing through my hand." Her face crumpled. "Sweetheart, what have you done? She'll kill you both now."

Sandra squeezed her hand. "She'll have to catch us first, all three of us."

"What do you mean?" Yvonne's brows rose and her ridges once more compressed.

Sandra's lips curved. "How would you like to see your daughter, Eva again, who you told me lives in Juniango?"

Yvonne shook her head back and forth. "I don't understand. How could that ever happen?"

Sandra knew the time had come to lay it all out. "We're going to leave together, you, me and Mastyr Griffin. I want you in the rose garden just after I deliver the meal to the Ruby Fae. Be there with anything you want to take with you because Griffin and I are leaving the camp as soon as I help the Ruby Fae to escape. And you're coming with us."

Griffin released Yvonne's hand then moved to stand in front of Sandra, his brow furrowed. "This won't work. Yvonne has already said they're hunting for me. It won't be long before they storm this place, especially if Margetta hears about it."

"She won't. Or if she does, she won't believe either of us is disloyal. She's odd that way. She thinks her slaves adore her."

Yvonne made a disgusted snort. "She's addled, that one."

"I'd have to agree." Griffin scrubbed a hand through his hair. "All right. So what are you proposing?"

"First," she turned to Yvonne. "Do you have the duplicate key to the tower room?" She smiled, because she'd already seen it in her vision.

"Yes, I do, but no one knows this." Yvonne's face lightened suddenly. A moment later, a smile lit her features. "I see what you're doing now." She chortled softly. "I'm in and I don't give a flying forest gremlin if I die tonight."

~ ~ ~

Griffin slowly paced Sandra's bedroom. He'd stayed behind because it would be one of the last places Fulton would be able to send troops to look for him. Fulton would need permission from Margetta herself to invade the women's quarters for whatever reason. But it chapped his hide to be forced to wait like this.

Yvonne and Sandra had agreed to say that they'd each seen him earlier in the fortress and that he'd finagled a beer from Yvonne. But he'd left some time ago, through the rose garden, heading to the quarters housing the female service slaves.

Setting Fulton on a wild goose chase was the best they could do and it might just work. If fate was on their side, they had a chance.

They were also of one mind, that no matter what, Regan must be given an opportunity to escape her imprisonment. A woman with so much power, once bonded to one of Margetta's loyal mastyr vampires, would become a formidable opponent in the final stages of the war. Griffin had no doubt Margetta would help force the bond, perhaps using a controlling spell to alter the Ruby Fae's good nature.

Timing was crucial, though. Griffin had to remain hidden in Sandra's room until the key was delivered with the next meal. If all went well, Sandra would be able to get the key to the Ruby Fae, after which Regan could escape the fortress. Then he would attempt to carry Sandra and Yvonne through the terrible mist spell and out of the Dauphaire Mountains.

But dawn was coming soon, as well as the appointed hour for Sandra's wraith-bonding ceremony.

They didn't have much time.

What concerned Griffin the most, however, was the mist he now saw from Sandra's window. Since he'd completed the blood rose bond with her, his increase in power had brought the mist fully within his vision. It appeared as a thick wall surrounding the entire camp, including all the space overhead. It was no wonder his previous escape attempts had failed.

But instinctively he knew there was a pathway through the spell. He'd sensed it before. And now that he was bonded with Sandra, its existence became fixed in his mind. The trouble was, he couldn't see it, at least not yet.

The lives of Both Yvonne and Sandra were on his shoulders now. But without the pathway, Margetta's spell might as well have been made of cement.

~ ~ ~

When the fat troll opened the door to the tower, Sandra walked in. The Ruby Fae stood near the small table and chairs, her hands folded in front of her. She looked composed and elegant, but she made no move to sit down nor did she speak to Sandra until the tower cell door closed and the lock turned in the grate.

Regan's gaze went almost immediately to the white towel rolled up beneath Sandra's arm. Sandra forced herself to remain calm, even though her heart beat so hard in her chest it was a pulse in her ears.

She didn't make eye contact with Regan, since the troll watched them both through the barred window in the door. She didn't want to give anything away at this late hour.

"As you requested last time, Mistress," Sandra said pointedly. "I brought an additional towel for you."

Regan, of course, had made no such request, but she responded in kind. "Thank you. I'm grateful you remembered. And how are you, Sandra?"

"Very well, thank you, Mistress." Her tone was breathy, as she slid her gaze to Regan and dipped her chin once.

She set the tray on the small table, then moved to the washstand, tucking the towel next to a basin and companion water pitcher. She'd dreaded dropping the towel for fear the key would tumble out and clink loudly on the stone floor. But the towel fit perfectly between the two ceramic pieces.

To Regan's credit, she appeared impassive. But Sandra caught the glitter in her eye as Regan sat down on the stool in front of the table.

Knowing it was important to stick to the habitual order of service, especially since the troll was still watching, Sandra moved each item off the tray in the same measured sequence as last time, though her fingers trembled slightly.

Regan held her hands together on her lap in a tight clasp. Her gaze seemed to be fixed to the braid draped over Sandra's left shoulder.

Regan's voice entered her mind. *You brought the key? It's in the towel, right?*

With her back to the door and therefore the prying eyes of the troll as well, Sandra met and held Regan's gaze. *I did.*

Because Sandra was also positioned to block the troll's view of Regan, she touched Sandra's arm. *Can you come with me? I'm a strong flyer.*

Sandra wanted to shake her head, but knew the troll would report even this small movement to Margetta. *I might have my own way out. But if not, do all you can to take this monster down.*

She watched the Ruby Fae's eyes fill with tears. *I will. May the Goddess be with you.*

And with you.

No other words were exchanged, though two tears rolled down Sandra's cheeks.

Sandra took the empty tray from off the table, and nodding to the troll through the barred window, she heard the key turn in the lock once more.

When the troll opened the door, Sandra moved into the small hallway beyond. She slowly made her way down the curved and very steep stairwell, her slippers shushing on the stone floor.

She offered a prayer to the Goddess to protect Regan and guide her as she made her escape from Margetta's fortress. The Ruby Fae's future was now out of her hands, but she hoped with all her heart Regan somehow found a way past Margetta's spell.

When she reached the hall that connected to both the outdoors and the fortress proper, she waited for the troll to open the door for her. She avoided eye-contact, which helped keep the troll's occasional advances to a minimum.

For a moment, when he made no move to open the door, she feared this would be one of those times she'd have to shout and threaten him. Mostly, he drank too much beer, as he had been tonight, and smelled like it.

She directed her thoughts to Griffin. *We're at the bottom of the tower. The guard is trying to decide whether to flirt with me or not.*

Do you need me to come to you?

Not sure. Let me talk to him first. She glanced at the troll and aloud said, "Well? Mistress Yvonne is waiting for me. And in case you've forgotten, I have a ceremony tonight. And I don't think Margetta would like it if you roughed me up just before she mate-bonded me to a wraith."

"Fuck," the troll spit. He huffed a sigh, wrinkled up his nose and pulled the door wide.

Sandra crossed the threshold and felt his hand graze her bottom. She turned toward him, nostrils flaring. "You sure you want to be touching me? Because remember, once I'm Invictus, I won't have any manners left and I might just feel the need to come after you."

He looked up at her like a hurricane had just hit his face. "Y-yes, Mistress. Apologies."

"Then make it up to me and carry the tray back to the kitchen. I'm going to freshen up in my room. Maybe then, I'll think of you with kindness."

He took the tray and moved down the hall, his slippered feet padding quickly. As a house slave, he was required to wear soft shoes. Margetta didn't like a lot of clunking in her home.

To Griffin, she pathed. *I'm on my way.*

Her heart once more set up a racket. She wondered if Regan had made her escape yet. From the tower cell, Regan could cross the roof of the fortress and levitate over the side, though how she was supposed to navigate Margetta's powerful spell, Sandra didn't know. But at least she'd provided the Ruby Fae with a chance to get out.

Griffin's voice slid through her mind. *Yvonne's not here yet.*

She's not? Okay. Something has prevented her. Yvonne should have returned to Sandra's bedroom by now. *I'll go to the kitchen and see what the trouble is.*

We're running out of time. Once you have her, let me know you're on your way and I'll meet you in the rose garden.

Will do.

Sandra ran down the servants' stairs as fast as she could, her skirts held in both hands. She was puffing by the time she reached the hall outside Yvonne's room. She heard Fulton shouting at her.

Needing an excuse to barge in, she ran the short distance to the supply room and gathered up a small basin, a towel and some soap.

She hurried back to the housekeeper's room and with Fulton still attempting to shout Yvonne down, she pushed the door wide. "I'm here for your feet, Mistress. Oh, hello, Mastyr Fulton. You'll forgive me, I don't have much time and I promised the housekeeper I'd tend to her corns before my bonding ceremony."

Fulton glanced down at the housekeeper's currently bare feet and recoiled at the sight of the knobby enflamed lumps on her toes. "Well, it'll have to wait. I have business here."

"Then you won't mind if I take care of Mistress's feet while you speak with her?"

"No. Yes. Who gives a fuck, and where is Mastyr Griffin?" His face had turned red.

Sandra shrugged. "How should either of us know? Isn't he your responsibility?" To Yvonne, she said, "I'll just fetch some warm water. I'll be right back. But remember, my bonding takes place in fifteen minutes."

Yvonne stared at her. "Thank you."

Sandra left the room and went into the kitchen. She needed to play this out and hopefully Fulton would get so frustrated, he'd leave. *Griffin?*

I'm here.

Fulton's in a state and has been harassing Yvonne in her room about you. I'm trying to get her out of there.

Let me know when you're ready. There's a commotion on the roof, by the way, and a number of Invictus pair are flying above the tower cell.

So the Ruby Fae was attempting her escape. Or maybe she'd already done it and was now long gone.

How do you think Margetta found out so fast? Margetta had never kept guards around the tower or on the roof.

Griffin was silent for a moment. *My guess is she might have had another spell in place, one to alert her if Regan left the tower. Though all the confusion might work in our favor right now. I'm looking at twenty wraith-pairs in the air. But hurry.*

I will.

With trembling fingers, she filled a tea kettle with hot water from a pot on the stove, added some cold water to cool it down then returned to the housekeeper's room.

Fortunately, Fulton was gone when Yvonne returned.

"You were brilliant. He left in a huff shortly after you said you were fetching water." Yvonne smiled. "But I think it was the sight of my ugly feet that did the trick."

"Why did you even have your slippers off?" She placed the tea kettle on the nearby table, setting it on a wood trivet.

At that, Yvonne offered a crooked smile. "I'd go naked from this place if I could because I don't intend to take anything with me. Not a damn thing. I'll wear this gown, however, mostly because I don't want to scare off Mastyr Griffin." She even chuckled. "Now how about we do our disappearing act?"

These words eased Sandra's nerves a little. Yvonne seemed confident about their plan, or maybe she just didn't care what happened along the way. They were alike, each resigned to do what they could, but if the plan failed, so be it.

Sandra suggested they chat in quiet voices about the vegetable garden as they made their way to the entrance hall. That way if anyone was listening, nothing would appear to be out of the ordinary. Both Sandra and Yvonne had run-of-the-fortress privileges.

As it was, there were very few slaves about and the few they saw were heading to the north door to have a look at the commotion in the skies. Griffin was right; Regan's escape would work in their favor.

Once in the rose garden, Sandra alerted Griffin that she and Yvonne were in place.

Heading to the entrance hall now.

She then watched the frantic movements of the wraith-pairs flying above the fortress. She could also hear Margetta shouting orders for a large force to go in pursuit. Although, given that dawn was less than an hour away, Sandra didn't think the wraith-pairs would be able to accomplish very much.

She held Yvonne's hand as together they fixed their gazes to the sky.

Yvonne whispered. "We did it, didn't we? We got the key to the Ruby Fae."

She squeezed Yvonne's hand. "Yes, we did. And my senses tell me she got away."

Now, with a little luck, she and Yvonne could make their own escape, along with Griffin. But what remained unknown was how they were to break through Margetta's spell.

As Sandra continued to watch the dark night sky, she began to see the containment spell, like a wall of fog forming a massive shield above the fortress, as well as the camp and the surrounding forest. Doubts rose in a heavy swell through her heart. How were they supposed to escape now?

The door to the entrance hall opened and Griffin appeared. Shutting the door behind him, he started to move in their direction, when a man's voice called out, "So you've been hiding behind the skirts of a couple of stupid women."

Sandra whirled and watched Fulton appear at the hedge entrance to the garden, a dagger in one hand and his red battle energy glowing in his right palm. And he wasn't alone. Two more vampires, each a mastyr, moved into the space to flank him.

Instinctively, she wrapped her arms around Yvonne, shielding her. And without giving it a second thought, she levitated them swiftly down the gravel path to the west, getting them both to safety. One glance at Griffin told her he was ready to battle the vampire who had made his life hell for the past year.

Chapter Five

Griffin had seen Fulton beat slaves to death then hide their bodies from Margetta. He was a mean sonofabitch. And he wasn't even bonded to a wraith yet.

The men who flanked him weren't much better. Griffin had been at the receiving end of their fists as well as a variety of weapons over the past twelve months. If Margetta hadn't insisted on keeping Griffin alive, he would have been long dead, something he'd craved the first months of his captivity.

He knew what Fulton wanted and Griffin was ready.

He slowly moved in the bastard's direction, stepping down from the front stone step and along the gravel path. The rose bushes gave way to a broad stretch of grass, thirty feet to the hedge where Fulton and his men stood. He stopped at the edge of the lawn and waited.

Griffin's battle energy flowed in hot waves across his shoulders, down his arms and into both hands. The vibrations were more powerful than anything he'd previously experienced. At the same time, he felt his connection to Sandra and that so much of his new strength came from their shared bond.

I'm with you, Griffin. Whatever you need, I'm here. Just take him down. He's hurt so many of the slaves in the fortress.

That's the plan.

Griffin fixed his gaze on Fulton. "How about we finish this?"

Fulton glanced at Sandra then back to Griffin. "You think I don't know what's going on here? The moment Sandra showed up in the housekeeper's room, I could smell the nature of her blood and that she'd become something new. But I also felt the bond and since you'd already admitted to fucking the bitch, I figured out the rest. She's a blood rose, isn't she? And right now, you think you're going to leave the fortress alive." He shook his head with a cruel smile on his lips. "But I have other plans. I'm going to end your sorry life, then take Sandra for myself. And I won't be gentle."

Having bonded with Sandra, Griffin's life had shifted completely and dying was no longer on his priority list. The opposite was true. Love had changed everything for him.

What he hadn't figured out was how to defeat all three men and do it fast. Despite his increase in power, he knew he couldn't battle all of them by himself.

What lived inside him now, however, because he was bonded to a blood rose, went far beyond the nature of power. As he opened himself up to that bond, he finally realized he was connected to something greater than himself.

Sandra, I need you to access the blood rose bond. There's something here we can achieve together. My gut tells me your expanding fae abilities can enhance the situation.

I'm on it.

~ ~ ~

Sandra held Yvonne's hand. The troll was trembling, yet kept her chin high. She'd tangled with Fulton more than once herself.

"Yvonne, I'm going to concentrate on my faeness, but I'll need to release your hand."

Yvonne nodded, letting go of Sandra's hand. To Sandra's surprise, Yvonne then placed her hand on Sandra's shoulder. It was such a gentle supportive gesture, that somehow it sparked her fae power. Suddenly, the future flew around her once more in the same odd pieces, like a torn up photo.

Now, however, her fae instincts told her the collected picture would be important. She realized in that moment, because she was a blood rose bonded to a mastyr vampire, she was no longer a simple fae. She'd become something more, much more.

Hearing Fulton's vile threats also spurred her on.

Griffin would battle with all his might. She knew that and she could feel his battle energy vibrating heavily in the air. He wasn't the kind of man to hold back and he would do everything within his power to save her as well as Yvonne.

Yet it wouldn't be enough, not to vanquish all three vampires. She quickly began gathering the images into a cohesive portrait. Once it was complete, it became a steady flow beginning right where Griffin was standing and moving through what looked like a video of the battle start to finish.

If Griffin had that information, he'd know what to do and when to do it.

The next moment, just like the rolling vision, Griffin erected a heavy blue shield in front of him, extending it to cover both Sandra and Yvonne. But it wouldn't last, not when all three vampires began pummeling his shield with their corresponding red power.

Griffin. I've seen the battle, each of their moves.

What do you mean?

I've seen how the battle progresses. The bond has strengthened my blood rose ability and my power to access the future. I've seen how the battle can unfold in a way for you to defeat them. And I think I can send it to you.

She felt Griffin deliberate, but only for a moment. *Send it. Send it now. I know this is the way. And while I'm doing it, gather another image of our escape, or at least try. From the beginning, I sensed an escape route through Margetta's spelled mist. I have a gut feeling we need to find that pathway for all of us to survive and it will require split-second timing.*

I think you're right. So, here goes. While watching him, she held her telepathic channel wide open and brought the strange sequence of images forward, sending it swiftly into his mind.

His body jerked and at the same moment, Fulton gave the orders to burn down his shield. All three vampires let loose with even greater streams of their battle energies.

~ ~ ~

Griffin understood right away exactly what the images meant and how he could use them. There had been so many rumors about the blood rose bond that it was hard to know what to believe or not to believe.

But one of the accounts spoke exactly of this, the rise of new shared powers and the ability of the mastyr and his blood rose to work together to fight the enemy.

Whatever the case, with his battle shield still in place, he let the vision roll. It would slow as needed until he got a full picture of what he had to do. The battle would begin the moment he withdrew his shield.

He was fully aware that the activity overhead had died down and that soon he, Sandra and Yvonne would come under scrutiny. He had only a couple of minutes, if that, to get the women out of the fortress and past Margetta's spell-shield.

Yet, more than at any other time in his life, he was ready.

In a fast streak of movement, he transferred his full-shield energy into pulses from each hand. Following the vision now playing through his mind, he sent hard swift streaks from each of his palms, directing them at the enemy's red battle streams. He couldn't believe how fast he'd made this happen. Explosions erupted and one of the vampires flew backward into the hedge screaming. One down.

Fulton threw an axe, which Griffin dodged with a quick lateral levitation because of the telepathic video. A split second later, the remaining vampire, Brayer, sent a pulse of battle power at Griffin. He met it with one of his own, sending a shower of combined blue and red sparks high into the air.

Fulton then ran at him, dagger in hand. At the same time, Brayer sent another series of battle energy pulses at Griffin.

Griffin fired back at Brayer and because of the images in his head he knew what Fulton meant to do. With precision timing and still holding his battle stream steady at Brayer, Griffin levitated and came down with a scissors grip around Fulton's neck. Brayer withdrew his battle energy at the same time, otherwise he'd hit Fulton.

Griffin then somersaulted, flinging Fulton onto his back on the grass. Fulton's dagger fell several feet away.

The images flowed, showing Griffin the angle of Brayer's next attack. Griffin levitated swiftly and grabbed Fulton's dagger. He whirled and arced in another levitation, meeting Brayer midair.

Griffin swiped the dagger across Brayer's abdomen, gutting him. Brayer screamed and fell on his side.

Griffin knew Fulton was already rising to his feet, his battle energy vibrating heavily.

Levitating and shifting to a horizontal position again, Fulton's battle energy pulsed harmlessly into the rose bushes. At the same moment, Griffin moved like a shot in Fulton's direction then dragged the blade over his throat.

Fulton clutched at his neck, dropped to his knees, then collapsed on the grass, blood spewing between his fingers.

All three vampires were down.

Griffin didn't hang around to make sure each made it to the afterlife. He had a tougher job to do right now, and his gut told him he only had a matter of seconds to escape the mist overhead.

At almost the same moment, Sandra's new vision, of their escape path through Margetta's mist, flowed into his head. In it, he saw wraith-pairs coming toward him in the garden. He didn't look back to see if they were actually there; he felt it in his bones.

He levitated away from them and swept in Sandra and Yvonne's direction. They were both ready and waiting for him, each with an arm extended high.

While still in flight, he caught Sandra with his right arm and Yvonne with his left, pulling them tight to his sides, grateful for his natural Guardsman strength. Neither woman uttered a sound as he carried them into the air at a phenomenal speed.

He pathed to both at the same time. *I've got you. Stay calm if you can. We're in Margetta's spell now.*

He had to slow to navigate the spell, but the pathway out of the mist was as clear to him as if he'd built it himself.

~ ~ ~

The mist clung to Sandra, a fae itch on her skin. She could feel Margetta's magic tugging at them from all sides. But the vision held true of the exact path Griffin needed to take. He flew slowly right now, easing left, then right, then back, always in motion.

Do you feel that, Griffin? The pull of the spell?

I do, but we're almost there.

Suddenly, Griffin burst past the mist and into the night sky. He went fast once more, flying like a rocket, arcing northeast.

They'd made it.

Griffin had used the path her blood rose ability had forged, and they'd made it out.

"We're free!" she shouted.

Yvonne, to Sandra's surprise, let out a loud whoop as well, that resounded over the Dauphaire Mountains below.

"I'm going to ease each of you onto one of my boots, give us all a little more stability. Yvonne, you first."

Sandra felt the slight shift sideways as Griffin adjusted the troll's feet.

"Your turn, Sandra."

He hefted her up with his extraordinary vampire strength until she was able to settle her feet on his right boot. She began to relax.

Griffin sustained his speed as they flew. The man was determined to get them to safety. Plus, they were running out of the cover of the night. It would be dawn in less than a half hour.

"Thank you, Sandra. Your timing was perfect. And the path you were able to detect through the spell was exactly what we needed to escape. We couldn't have done this otherwise. You did this for us."

She reached her arm over Griffin's shoulders and settled her hand on Yvonne's arm. "We're free, Mistress. We're free!"

"Yes, we are." This time, Yvonne's voice was much softer and Sandra was pretty sure she heard the former fortress housekeeper issuing a couple of solid sobs.

Sandra's throat grew tight as well. She'd spent thirty years serving a monster, watching fellow-slaves tortured and killed, or those that survived, bonded to wraiths. Yvonne had been in the fortress twice as long.

Then Griffin had arrived and now she was flying above the snow peaks of the Dauphaires.

Yvonne asked, "Where are we headed?"

Griffin's deep voice hit the air once more. "To Juniango to find your daughter, Eva, of course."

Sandra smiled and her heart swelled. She had a good man and she knew it.

This time, Yvonne didn't hold anything back and she wailed into the cool, early morning air. She was so lost in her emotions that her shaking caused all three of them to rattle around a bit. It was both poignant and amusing at the same time.

Griffin, you've done such an incredible thing tonight. And I hope more than anything we find Eva alive and well.

I know that you're the fae in our partnership, but my instincts tell me we will. Maybe I got that from you.

Well, for heaven's sakes don't tell her. She might really start to sob and send all three of us catapulting into a series of aerial somersaults we'd never recover from.

Oh, we'd recover.

His strong, masculine voice in her head and his confidence in his physical ability, worked on Sandra in a very female way. She caressed his back and shoulders. *Thank you. For everything.*

~ ~ ~

Griffin had a couple of bruises. That's all. Nothing serious as he flew Sandra and the good-hearted housekeeper toward the mountain village of Juniango.

He couldn't believe this had happened, this miracle of an escape. Fulton and his men would have taken him down had it not been for Sandra's strange gift and his own advanced abilities because he'd bonded with a blood rose.

He could recall one of the rumors that had made its way through the enslaved portion of the camp, talk involving the blood rose phenomenon. Many believed it had arisen specifically, coming from the Goddess herself, to counteract Margetta's intention to bring the Nine Realms under her control.

He knew one thing for certain: He couldn't have escaped the fortress without Sandra. He'd followed her video-like images to the letter, which had allowed him to defeat Fulton and his men as well as to navigate a very specific pathway through Margetta's mist. He'd always sensed there was an escape route through the Ancient Fae's spell, but he couldn't have found it by himself.

Yep, the whole thing was a blood rose miracle for which he'd be eternally grateful.

But Margetta's fortress wasn't the only thing he'd escaped. Until he'd met Sandra, and become her friend, his life had been a burned down forest where new growth would never take root. Battling for the past century had been his life, and he'd been happy to serve, built as he was for facing off with bad guys of any kind.

He was a protector and he'd been proud of it.

But he'd also been alone, suffering the effects of chronic pain, disconnected from all meaningful relationships except with his brothers-in-arms, and living his life on the outskirts of society.

Now, his life felt complete. He held a woman tight to his right side and he knew she'd stand with him no matter what happened in the coming days, weeks and years. She was that kind of woman.

He felt blessed beyond understanding and grateful beyond words.

He began his descent to the village of Juniango, his warrior eyes slowly searching for any sign of Invictus activity. Along Main Street, he saw several members of the Troll Brigade standing guard. Because dawn hadn't yet arrived, there were still a number of fae and vampires out, a few of them drunk and others finishing up some last minute shopping before being housebound the rest of the day.

He landed near the local pub, the Trollhead Inn, and carefully released his hold on Yvonne and Sandra. He didn't let go of either of them completely because for the uninitiated flight could cause dizziness.

Yvonne, especially, listed on her feet. "I'm so sorry, Mastyr, I don't know what's wrong with me."

"You're not used to flight. Let's go inside and have a pint. And if we need to, Sandra and I can spend the day here, in the inn."

She glanced up at the sign. "The Trollhead." She put a hand to her chest. "Am I home? Am I really home?"

Sandra was much steadier on her feet and left Griffin to join Sandra on her other side. She slid her arm around Yvonne's waist. "Come on. Let's have a drink then find out where your family is."

These words, however, caused the troll to put both hands to her face and burst into tears once more. Sandra, the good woman that she was, dipped down and surrounded the much shorter troll with both arms, holding her close.

While the women were speaking softly to each other and now weeping together, the door to the Trollhead opened. Griffin immediately stepped in front of the women, then lowered his knees and shoulders ready to face whatever opponent would come at him. He'd been sparring for so long with conscienceless freaks that this habit wasn't going to disappear any time soon.

What met his gaze, however, was the long leather, sleeveless coat of the Camberlaune Guard, thigh boots and leathers. And the red hair of one of his brothers-in-arms. "Owen?"

Owen stared at him unblinking for several seconds. "Griffin, holy fuck! I saw you last at Wayford. We thought you were dead! Where the hell have you been, you ugly bastard?"

The next moment, Owen's beefy arms surrounded him and the crushing tightness of the man-hug made his eyes burn and his throat ache. His thoughts had been all for the women, getting them to safety, and seeing if he could restore Yvonne to her family.

The last thing he'd expected was to run into a friend out here in Juniango.

When Owen pulled back, he slapped Griffin on the shoulder. "Damn, you're lean, but I see you've still worked out."

Yeah, he'd worked out, wielding weapons against the Invictus in practice sessions for the past year. He didn't say that. Instead, he explained where he'd been then gestured to Yvonne and Sandra. "We could use a drink."

Owen pulled him inside and called out to the troll bartender. "Four pints, Virginia. We've got some celebrating to do over here."

"Coming up, Big Guns." His nickname fit. Owen had a pair of massive biceps and played it up constantly. He'd left off wearing the woven Guardsman shirt as well, following Mastyr Ian's lead who headed up the Camberlaune Guard.

All four of them sat at a table. A moment later, Virginia brought brimming mugs over and passed them around.

Owen took a drink then got on his phone, ready to alert the rest of the Guard, but Griffin shut him down. "Don't. I know for a fact Margetta has a spy network in Camberlaune and I don't want anyone to know where we are. You good with that?"

Owen stared at him for a long moment. "Sweet Goddess, Griffin. Are you shitting me?"

He shook his head slowly. "I picked up a lot of information from the camp, but I'm not saying another word to you or anyone else until I speak with Mastyr Ian." Griffin took a long swig.

Owen's expression grew serious. "He's been hunting for the Ruby Fae this past month. We've hardly seen him. She's somewhere in the Dauphaire Mountains. Wait. Why are all three of you smiling at me? Oh, shit, you've seen her."

Griffin nodded. "And we're hopeful she escaped tonight. But you'll probably know more about that over the next twenty-four hours."

Virginia returned to the table to join in the conversation, then settled her gaze on Yvonne. "Wait a minute. I know you.

Aren't you Eva's mother, the one who disappeared? Why it has to be decades now."

Yvonne set her pint down and put both hands to her chest. She looked suddenly frightened, her lips pinched. "I am."

Griffin watched her swallow hard. He understood. She was afraid she'd be hearing bad news.

Virginia put a hand on her shoulder. "Eva lives around here, you know. She has a farm about ten miles east. And she just had another baby about a year ago, a little girl."

"She does? She did? Oh, my." More tears, then Yvonne turned to Griffin. She stared at him but didn't say a word.

He glanced toward the windows. The sky still wasn't light out, but he felt a strong warning vibration down his spine. When Sandra placed her hand on his arm and nodded her encouragement, he made his decision. "Get me directions. I can get us over there in time, but Sandra and I will have to spend the night in Eva's home." He finished his beer and shoved Owen from the booth.

Owen bear-hugged him again, as Virginia whipped her phone from her pocket and made the call. "No, Eva, they can't talk. They have to get airborne right now or you'll have a fried vampire on your hands as well as a blistered fae."

She ended the call and as they moved toward the door, Virginia told them how to get to the farm.

Griffin put his hand on Virginia's head. "Make picture in your mind."

"You can do that?" Virginia asked, eyes wide.

"Hell, yes."

Virginia closed her eyes and concentrated.

"Got it." To Sandra and Yvonne, he added, "This is going to be quick. Get ready."

The women trailed after him as he headed to the door. He heard Owen say to Virginia, "Dawn's coming. Looks like I'm going to have to spend the night here. Got an extra room?"

"Nope. But I've got a bed and you're welcome in it."

He heard Owen chuckle in that deep, rowdy way of his.

After listening to his brother-in-arms, Griffin was hit hard but in the best way that he'd made it out of the fortress alive. He was home.

He waved to Owen, and Owen lifted his chin then smiled.

Yeah, he was home.

Once outside, each woman hopped up on his foot and the moment he had them tight against his sides, he shot into the air. He could feel the dawn coming like a freight train.

~ ~ ~

Sandra's heart raced as Griffin flew north past Juniango and into a rolling countryside. She held Yvonne's hand across the broad stretch of Griffin's chest.

The trip took a whole fifteen seconds. Had to be a new record.

When Griffin began his descent, the housekeeper's grip on her hand increased. Sandra's heart thumped so loud that she felt as though she was the one coming home and not Yvonne.

Griffin landed fifteen feet from the front door on a gravel path. Pansies in a variety of colors had been planted by the scores on either side of the walkway. A well-kept winter lawn also showed the love and care of a serious gardener.

The front porch light came on and the door opened. A lovely female troll with a baby on her hip opened the door. Her lips were in a round 'o'. "Mama?"

"Eva!" the housekeeper cried as she stepped off Griffin's boot. She didn't lose her balance this time, not even a little. She ran to the woman and an embrace followed that soon had the baby crying.

Eva drew back and comforted the child. "We got the phone call from Juniango barely a minute ago. We all thought you were dead."

"Not dead. But after all this time, I wasn't even sure you'd remember me."

Eva looked shock, her complexion paling. "You're my mama. How could I ever forget you?"

More tears followed, including the baby's. But Griffin had to disrupt the reunion since he could feel the dawn pounding a warning inside his head.

Eva apologized profusely for keeping them standing outside, then invited them into her house.

A few minutes later, Sandra stood off to the side of the large living room, Griffin's arm around her, his hand on her waist. She leaned against his chest, his summery field scent giving her comfort.

It was a beautiful thing to be with him while she watched Yvonne and Eva sitting side by side on the couch, hands clasped tightly together. Each smiled with tears brimming and rolling. Sixty years had passed since mother and daughter had seen each other.

Eva's husband sat across from them, holding their most recent offspring in his arms. The one-year-old had fallen asleep in his arms. Yvonne's son-in-law was a handsome troll with brown hair combed straight back.

As the sun rose, Sandra remained safely in the house with Griffin, away from direct sunlight. Eva's extended family began to arrive. Sandra greeted and received the thanks of Eva's grown children and their spouses and what were Yvonne's grandchildren and even a few great-grandchildren.

The house quickly grew crowded and before long a full-blown celebration was in progress. Neither Sandra nor Griffin could leave the shelter of the home, but the trolls had free rein of the outdoors and the barbecues soon lit up.

Food began to arrive as well, slabs of meat ready for the grill, all sorts of salads, and chips, a plethora of home-made berry pies, and an obligatory keg of beer.

The homecoming brought tears to Sandra's eyes more than once. She didn't have a family of her own, nor did Griffin, one of the reasons perhaps they'd been able to relate to each other so well. Each was essentially an orphan in the Realm world. But when Eva's husband moved to sit beside his wife, their daughter still asleep on his shoulder, other memories intruded.

She put a hand to her mouth and turned into Griffin.

What is it?

I had a family once.

He rubbed her back, but for a long time didn't say anything. Finally, he moved through her mind gently, *I'll be your family now, Sandra. And maybe, if the Goddess wills, we'll have babies of our own and can create a dynasty as Yvonne has.*

She drew back a little and looked up at him. *Those might be the best and sweetest words you could have ever said to me.*

He leaned down and kissed her. Sandra was pretty sure he'd meant only to offer comfort. But the moment his lips touched hers, a profound longing rolled through her to be alone with him.

He drew back, a frown between his light blue eyes. *I need to be with you.*

I was thinking the exact same thing. Maybe I was feeling your desire as much as my own. She glanced around. *Do you think we'd be missed if we retired to our room? Although, it looks like most of the party has moved outside.*

I'm sure it'll be fine. Besides, this has been a long night and I think both of us could use some sleep. His lips curved. *And I know I could use a shower.*

When he released her, Sandra was going to search for either Eva or Yvonne when the latter moved back into the house from the kitchen door.

Sandra drew close. "We're feeling the need to retire."

Yvonne nodded and ordered the rest of the friends and family in the house to join everyone else outside. Once they'd disappeared into the backyard, Yvonne extended her hands to them. Sandra took one, Griffin the other.

"I have no words, except thank you." Her eyes grew watery once more as she drew first Sandra's fingers to her lips and kissed them, then Griffin's.

With pinched lips, she nodded to each, and once more said, "Thank you."

She then released their hands with a definitive jerk as though working hard to control her emotions. "Earlier, I told Eva you'd both need your sleep soon. In her basement, is a room she keeps on hand for any of the Camberlaune Guardsmen who might get caught out here too close to dawn. She had two of her daughters make up the room for you. You'll both be safe through the day, and there's a proper bed for your Guardsman stature." She waved a hand up and down Griffin's six-five frame.

Sandra smiled. "Thank you so much, Yvonne. And thank your daughter for us."

"Yes," Griffin added. "Add my thanks as well."

"Of course. And now I have something for you to take to your room." She drew a tray from the back counter. "In the middle of all the bustle, I prepared you a meal." She handed the tray to Sandra. "There's a mini-fridge downstairs as well, so help yourself to anything that's inside."

It felt so familiar to take the tray from the fortress housekeeper. How many times had Yvonne handed them to her over the years? Thousands.

Yvonne met and held her gaze, then nodded slowly, her lips curving into a soft smile. "I guess this is our last tray."

Tears brimmed in Sandra's eyes. "I guess it is."

Yvonne once more wiped her eyes. "Sleep well and we'll see you at full dark if not before. The Troll Brigade will be patrolling through the day here at Eva's farm, so you've nothing to worry about. And now, I'm rejoining my family." She waved once then slipped through the door to rejoin her family.

The stairs leading to the basement were near the front door. Sandra led the way, tray in hand. Griffin offered to carry it for her, but for some reason, maybe because it was the last one Yvonne would ever give her to carry, she wanted to complete the task.

But Griffin preceded her down the stairs, moving slowly. He didn't want her to fall and told her to mind her gown. It was so sweet, but unnecessary. She'd carried trays to all parts of the fortress through the years and if she slipped she'd glide into levitation.

At the bottom of the steps, the landing space was surprisingly roomy and tall enough for Griffin's Guardsman height. Clearly the home had been built to accommodate all species.

A table and two large chairs had been laid with a linen cloth and a small vase of roses set in the middle. The large, Guard-sized bed sat against the far wall with a bathroom off to the left. It was an excellent sleeping room for species caught out in the open at dawn.

Griffin stood very still, staring at the table. "This is incredibly thoughtful."

Sandra agreed. "It is."

Yet somehow she wasn't surprised. Eva was, after all, her mother's daughter.

Sandra asked Griffin to sit down and in the same way she'd served the Ruby Fae, she set everything out in the usual order. In an odd way, she felt as though she was saying good-bye to her time in the fortress.

She then brought two bottles of dark ale from the mini-fridge and placed them in front of Griffin. "I need your strength to get these twist caps off, which I hate with a passion."

He chuckled and with barely any effort at all, he opened the beers.

She sat down and took the bottle he offered to her. He didn't drink right away, but held his up. "To the woman I never believed possible."

She smiled. "And to the man who controlled my dreams for months."

His eyes crinkled as he laughed and the furrow between his brows softened. For a moment, she could see all the way into the future, to a man who eventually learned how to breathe a little. She knew she would ease him in that way as he would gentle down her grief.

He clinked bottles with her, then she took a swig, joining him.

After enjoying a meal of cold cuts and a spicy potato salad, with a few red pepper strips on the side, Sandra took her shower first. She made liberal use of the lavender-scented soap, grateful to have a strong floral fragrance to replace the old fortress smell.

When she was done, she wrapped a towel around her body, but found neatly folded stack of clothes sitting on the counter.

She opened the door slightly and saw Griffin sitting at the table, a book in his hand. "You're reading?"

He nodded and held up the cover for her to see. It appeared to be a book on the oceans of the Nine Realms. "Something I haven't done in a long time." He was frowning. He'd lost a year of his life and probably wondered what else he'd missed.

"Question. What are these clothes?"

He glanced into the bathroom. She was partially hidden behind the door. "Oh. Right. Eva brought them down. She'd sent a request out to her family and neighbors on your behalf. She guessed at your size. She said not to worry if nothing fits. She'd have more for you to try on this evening."

"I'll be out in a sec."

"Take your time."

She closed the door, needing a moment. She was completely overwhelmed. The styles had changed a lot in thirty years, but the garments were basic; bra, underwear, shirts and jeans. And at the bottom of the pile was a beautiful, dark green floor-length negligee.

For some reason the sight of it made her burst into tears. This was essentially her first night as Griffin's bonded blood rose and the thought she could be normal and have something pretty to wear for him, turned her inside out.

After a moment, she pulled herself together and splashed water on her face. She brushed out her long, damp, red hair and brushed her teeth; everything had been provided for them. She was grateful beyond words.

She slid into the negligee and though it was snug across her breasts, the rest fit her like a glove. Besides, she was pretty sure Griffin wouldn't mind the splendid show of cleavage.

When she was better composed, she opened the door. Griffin glanced at her, his gaze sliding head to toe, and immediately stood up. He set his book down on the table, and moved toward her. "You look beautiful. Was this in the clothes I set on the sink?"

She nodded. "Yes, but it's a little tight."

He growled softly, holding her arms in a gentle clasp as his gaze fell to her breasts. "It's perfect."

He released her almost immediately. "But you're clean and I'm not."

He kissed her once on the lips, then headed into the bathroom, closing the door.

Sandra felt oddly nervous, like a bride on her honeymoon. She moved around the bedroom. She placed the tray outside the door with the dishes arranged neatly on top. She drew the beautiful handmade quilt back, folding it in several neat rows, then let it fall onto the bench at the end of the bed. She plumped the two large pillows. She even brought the flowers over to the nightstand, then took them back to the table, then returned them to the nightstand.

She put a hand to her chest, trying to tell herself to calm down and that's when she realized two things. First, her heart was laden, which meant she'd made a new supply for her man, for Griffin, because she was his blood rose. And second, the nerves she felt weren't just her own.

She sat down on the side of the bed and chuckled. She could feel Griffin and how much his excitement and anxiety matched her own.

When Griffin finally emerged from the bathroom, he had a towel around his waist. His long hair was wet, but he'd combed it straight back so that his strong cheekbones angled to form beautiful, masculine planes.

She rose to her feet.

"I can feel you," he said.

She nodded, her lips curving. "I'm oddly nervous."

"Me, too."

"We've made love twice, Griffin, so why am I trembling?"

He drew close and planted his hands on her hips. "Because it's a lot more than anxiety. I'm feeling your love for me at the same time and your excitement about being back in bed with me, and something more, like you're smiling at the future." He petted her head, then pushed her hair behind her ear. "I used to love seeing your braid dangling over your shoulder. Sweet Goddess, the sight of you first thing each evening filled me with hope."

"I felt the same way. I couldn't wait for you to arrive in the slaves' dining hall."

He smiled. "You always saved a place for me."

"Of course I did. You were my best friend and now, well, you're everything."

He cupped the back of her neck and kissed her.

Sandra slid her hands up his arms. She could feel two sensations at once, how her touch felt to Griffin and the smooth strength of his biceps.

She parted her lips for him, savoring this first connection of his tongue in her mouth, sliding in and out, making a wonderful promise.

But what was this like for Griffin? All of it?

~ ~ ~

Griffin drew back, staring into luminous green eyes. Love swelled his heart, a completely foreign sensation. He was bonded to this woman as well, married to her, though the ceremony was yet to come. "I love you." His voice was only a whisper.

"Make love to me, Griffin." She caressed his face and kissed him. "I never thought I'd have a husband again. And maybe one day, we'll have a family together, just as you said."

Her words washed over him like an enormous wave, cleansing him from the dark past of his solitary life, of his imprisonment serving as a sparring partner for Margetta's army, and from his guilt that his participation was a betrayal of his brothers-in-arms.

He started to lift her, but she stopped him with a smile and a hand on his chest. "We should get rid of a couple things first." When she slid her hands into the tucked-in waist of the towel, his thigh muscles and abdomen tightened.

Pulling the towel apart, she let it fall to the floor. She touched him afterward, caressing his cock with her hand, then kissed him.

When she drew back, his gaze fell to her cleavage. He leaned down and took his time kissing his way to the silky green fabric.

He didn't stay too long. "Yeah, this needs to go." He chuckled softly and grabbed the hem of her negligee, pulling it up and over her head. He let it fall to the floor on top of his towel.

He lifted her, cradling her in his arms, then gently laid her out on the bed.

As he stretched out on top of her, he kissed her for a long time, then drew back. "You're a beautiful woman, Sandra, inside and out. And I love you with all my heart."

She returned his gaze, her eyes warm with affection. Her hands caressed his shoulders then his arms. "Can you believe we found something so wonderful in the horror of Margetta's fortress?"

He shook his head, treasuring all that she was as his bonded blood rose. "It will be a beautiful story we tell our children and their children."

He made love to her taking his time and hoping that the block walls insulated by the earth, would keep their shared moans from reaching too many ears.

He hardly cared. What meant something to him was giving Sandra pleasure in as many ways as he could. When he finally released his seed into her, his hope was that it would take root and begin the family that would anchor them in Camberlaune for the rest of their long-lived lives.

~ ~ ~

Two weeks later, Sandra stood on the front porch of the home Griffin had owned prior to his abduction. Mastyr Ian, ruler of Camberlaune Realm, had taken custody of the house when Griffin had been abducted. His intention had been to one day return the house to Griffin, should he escape whatever bondage Margetta had placed him in. Or in the event he learned of Griffin's death, to give the home to the Camberlaune Fae Guild to use as they saw fit.

When Griffin had finally met with Ian directly and shared the details of his captivity as well as the size of Margetta's army, Ian had welcomed him home and given him the keys to the house. Griffin had wanted to immediately rejoin the Guard, but Ian had insisted he take at least two weeks to be with his blood rose.

Griffin hadn't protested very much, and for that, Sandra was grateful. The more she was with him, the more she craved him. In many ways, this had been their honeymoon.

She felt more connected to him than ever.

Griffin's home was in the outskirts of the city of Mercata, in the foothills of the Venaset Mountains. Situated on an elevation, Sandra looked out at the glittering city lights of Mercata, clouded ever so slightly with her own spelled mist. Now that she'd advanced in power, she'd begun serious spellcasting especially those designed for protection. Griffin's property was now cloaked and only the most powerful Realm-folk would be able to detect its existence. Certainly, very few Invictus pairs could ever get through the spell. If they reached it, they'd be turned back with an overwhelming sense they'd gone the wrong way.

Her fae senses told her clearly that she and Griffin were in no way a priority for Margetta.

"Sandra, where are you?" Griffin sounded like he was in the back of the house, maybe as far as the master bedroom. Their home was a single story and had every modern convenience. But it was fairly large and the distance from the front door to the bedroom was a nice trek.

"I'm on the front porch, envisioning how I want to re-landscape the slope to the driveway. Are you about ready?" She'd fed him, of course, because this would be his first night back battling the Invictus as a Guardsman.

"I'll be there in a minute," he called back.

She felt completely torn about his leaving. She wanted him home with her and she wanted him safe. But she'd married a fighting man and knew he had to do all that he could to keep the Realm-folk of Camberlaune safe. He'd also gown antsy over the past few days. He needed to be with his brother's-in-arms. The war was heating up and rumors were flying everywhere that Mastyr Stone of Tannisford Realm was engaged in organizing a major offensive against the Ancient Fae. Very soon, Ian would head to Tannisford for a meeting with all the ruling mastyrs of the Nine Realms.

A week ago, when Sandra and Griffin had shared a meal with Mastyr Ian and the Ruby Fae, Sandra had felt the depth of Ian's sadness over the loss of his second-in-command, Mastyr Ben. He'd served as Mastyr Ian's right-hand-man for over half a millennium. Griffin had been shocked, having considered Ben one of his closest friends.

But there'd been another layer that had felt like betrayal to Sandra. She would probably never know what really happened, but her fae senses told her Ben's death had been necessary, which made her feel sick in a way that had caused Griffin to offer a questioning brow. She'd shaken her head, doubting she would share her concerns with him. Because of the hurt in Ian's eyes, she'd also avoided asking any other questions about Mastyr Ben.

Reuniting with Regan had been an amazing experience and a very long hug had followed along with a few dozen tears shed by them both. Regan had thanked her over and over for her bravery in getting the tower cell key to her.

Of course, Regan had known at the outset of their reunion that Sandra had become a blood rose much in the same way Sandra could detect the similar power within Regan. A long conversation had followed, separate from the men, about what it was to be a blood rose and the tremendous intimacy that had followed. The men had stood side-by-side across the room, each drinking tumblers of whisky. She'd heard snippets of their conversation, but it was all about the war and the coming meeting in Tannisford.

Because Griffin had risen in his mastyr power, he was now second-in-command of the Camberlaune Vampire Guard. When Ian left for Tannisford, Griffin would serve in Ben's place.

And tonight was his return to the Guard.

It helped a lot to have a fellow blood rose to talk with.

So much had changed in thirty years, including the advent of the Internet which hadn't been available to any of the slaves in the fortress. Sandra was presently on a crash course and spent most of her time online bringing herself up-to-speed.

She heard the sound of Griffin's boots on the tiled floor behind her. She turned to smile at him and her breath caught all over again.

He wore the traditional sleeveless, leather Guardsman coat, along with a brand new pair of the absurdly sexy thigh boots and pants. Like Ian, he didn't wear a shirt and Sandra just about melted at the sight of his heavily muscled arms.

His smile grew wicked and he lowered his chin as he moved, which gave him that caveman look she'd come to love. If he hadn't been heading out, she would have taken his hand and hauled him back to bed.

Instead, she worked at controlling her desire for him and put a hand to her chest, trying to get her heart to calm down.

When he drew close, he put his hands on her hips, something he liked to do. "I'm feeling your desire and it's not helping me at all." But he chuckled as he spoke.

And she of course took the opportunity to fondle his muscled arms. She sometimes felt guilty about how much she loved his body. But when she told him, he'd laughed and gotten a really affectionate look in his eye. 'I'm all yours, babe. Every last bit of me.' That's what he'd said.

She leaned up and kissed him, a long passionate kiss to remind him what he could look forward to when he returned.

As she drew back, it took every ounce of strength not to beg him to stay home with her. But she was a warrior's wife now, and it was important to let him know she supported his service as a protector of Camberlaune Realm.

She waved to him as he took off into the night sky, heading to Somerstrong and the Vampire Guard's Communication Center.

She stayed on the front step until she could no longer see him. He'd be back before dawn and she'd count the hours until he was safe in bed beside her once more.

She remained on the porch for a long time after, drinking in the freedom her love for Griffin had brought her. Her grief for her lost family had finally abated in the arms of her warrior bond-mate. And in return, she'd given him a life without the crippling pain that all mastyr vampires endured.

Nothing could make her happier, except perhaps one thing.

She smiled as she placed a hand on her lower abdomen. She could feel the life already growing in her belly. She wondered if Griffin had felt it as well, or if this was her secret to share when she was ready.

Griffin's promise that he would make a family with her had come true. The bounty of life, of the Goddess's enormous love for her and for Griffin, poured down on her in waves of sheer joy.

Love in the Fortress

She'd been given a double portion with Griffin, and she would savor every moment she had with him, now and forever.

Thank you for reading **LOVE IN THE FORTRESS**! In our new digital age, authors rely on readers more than ever to share the word. Here are some things you can do to help!

Sign up for my newsletter! You'll always have the *latest releases and coolest contests*! http://www.carisroane.com/contact-2/

Leave a review! You've probably heard this a lot lately and wondered what the fuss is about. But reviews help your favorite authors -- A LOT -- to become visible to the digital reader. So, anytime you feel moved by a story, leave a short review at your favorite online retailer. And you don't have to be a blogger to do this, just a reader who loves books!

Enter my latest contest! I run contests all the time so be sure to check out my contest page today! **ENTER NOW!** http://www.carisroane.com/contests/

Now Available: EMBRACE THE HUNT, Book 8 of the Blood Rose Series

A powerful vampire warrior. A beautiful fae of great ability. A war that threatens to destroy their love for the second time…

http://www.carisroane.com/8-embrace-the-hunt/

Be sure to check out the Blood Rose Tales Box Set – TRAPPED, HUNGER, and SEDUCED -- shorter works for a quick, sexy, satisfying read. For more information: http://www.carisroane.com/blood-rose-tales-box-set/

Also, be sure to check out the Blood Rose Tales – TRAPPED, HUNGER, and SEDUCED -- shorter works set in the world of the Blood Rose, for a quick, satisfying read.

BLOOD ROSE TALES BOX SET

http://www.carisroane.com/blood-rose-tales-box-set/

About the Author

Caris Roane is the New York Times bestselling author of thirty paranormal romance books. Writing as Valerie King, she has published fifty novels and novellas in Regency Romance. Caris lives in Phoenix, Arizona, loves gardening, enjoys the birds and lizards in her yard, but really doesn't like scorpions!

www.carisroane.com

You can find me at:

Website (http://www.carisroane.com/)
Blog (http://www.carisroane.com/journal/)
Facebook (https://www.facebook.com/pages/Caris-Roane/160868114986060)
Twitter (https://twitter.com/carisroane)
Newsletter (http://www.carisroane.com/contact-2/)

Author of:

Guardians of Ascension Series (http://www.carisroane.com/the-guardians-of-ascension-series/) – **Warriors of the Blood crave the *breh-hedden***

Dawn of Ascension Series (http://www.carisroane.com/dawn-of-ascension-series/) – **Militia Warriors battle to save Second Earth**

Rapture's Edge Series (http://www.carisroane.com/raptures-edge/) – **Militia Warriors, Luken and Endelle battle to save Third Earth**

Blood Rose Series (http://www.carisroane.com/the-blood-rose-series/) – **Only a blood rose can fulfill a mastyr vampire's deepest needs**

Blood Rose Tales (http://www.carisroane.com/blood-rose-tales-series/) – **Short tales of mastyr vampires who hunger to be satisfied**

Men in Chains Series (http://www.carisroane.com/men-in-chains-series/) – **Vampires struggle to get free of their chains and save the world**

The Flame Series (http://www.carisroane.com/flame-series/) – **Vampires battle it out with witches for control of their world**

CPSIA information can be obtained
at www.ICGtesting.com
Printed in the USA
FSOW02n1105090217
30618FS